murder anonymous

murder
anonymous

by Anthony Gilbert, PSEUD.

Lucy Beatrice Malleson

 RANDOM HOUSE: New York

murder
anonymous

i ◇◇

THE FIERCE AND sullen day was burning out in a sudden glow of splendor. Behind the fortressed Pennines, dark with rain, the horizon blazed with a white radiance. Ragged bunches of cloud, moving across the torn sky, assumed mysterious shapes. Although no one, except cattle who had no choice, appeared to be abroad, the world seemed densely peopled. Mr. Crook came sailing over the peak of a dark hill and looked down into the valley. Once the light had faded, it was like looking into a pit of blackness. For what appeared to be hours he had been driving through the sodden Fells. Here and there in the black nest beneath him a light gleamed, as strange as a fallen star. He presumed these lights indicated dwellings—nothing so civilized as a street lamp could be anticipated here, he reminded himself. How the inhabitants of these scattered cottages got about, unless they were mysteriously winged, he couldn't imagine. No car, he was convinced, could negotiate those rutted lanes.

"Wouldn't surprise me if I'd driven through the end of the world into the kingdom of the Wizard of Oz," he remarked aloud. A car with less heart than the old Superb would have folded up before this, but she had plowed resolutely through mud, over boulders, skirted ditches, and done everything except fly the hedgerows. He put her into low gear and started the descent into the valley.

Only the burning need to find a piece of missing evidence for a client whose chances were rather less than those of the average outsider would have dragged Crook more than half across England. He saw the horses and cows huddled under dripping trees, manes streaky with rain, so far gone they scarcely bothered to

3

look up as he approached. One more blessing to add to my list, Arthur Crook reflected. I could have been born a horse, and if he had, it wouldn't have been a Derby winner, he hadn't got the figure for that. It shouldn't happen to a dog, he told them sympathetically, tooling by. He had a map, but all these secondary roads, as courtesy compelled him to describe them, looked alike on such a night. He thought nostalgically of his eyrie of a flat in overcrowded Earls Court. The landlord had insisted on doing it up after the war, and a cleaner called in at irregular intervals, but a stranger wouldn't have believed a decorator (still less a woman) had set foot inside it for forty years. A convict wouldn't have thanked him for his bed, and a rag-and-bone man would have expected to be paid to cart away his furniture, but to Crook it was the nearest place to heaven, short of the real thing, that he could conceive.

Presently the road branched. In any civilized district there would be a signpost here, but if there'd ever been one it had been uprooted by the wind or vandals, or someone had fancied it to build a fire. He stopped the Superb and took a coin out of his pocket. So far as he could see there was absolutely nothing to choose between the two roads. Heads left, tails straight on, he decided. The coin said heads, so he turned the car and drove in that direction. If he'd never known what he might have run into if he'd followed his nose, he certainly hadn't the least conception of the effect on his own future of this arbitrary way of deciding his course.

He had been moving decorously for a mile or more when he came to the house. Unlike the cottages and farms he had seen hitherto, it was actually sited on the road, with a pair of big wrought-iron gates enclosing a curving drive. It was a sizable-looking affair, but already he had realized that in this part of the country big houses didn't necessarily imply a big household. Only the well-to-do could afford the small compact properties with mod. cons. Already he'd seen great mansions that made him think of the House of Usher, inhabited by one aging lady, who had come there when she married perhaps forty years earlier, had brought up her children, watched them go into the world, buried her husband and stayed on because this was home, and loneliness in the Fells had quite a different connotation from the loneliness you found in the towns. Drawing nearer, his heart leaped up like the poet's—one of the Lakeland poets at that—to see, not a rainbow in the sky, but a light shining through a crack in the drawn curtain at an upper window. It was rather a faint light, probably hadn't even got electricity, he thought resignedly, but it was there. He stopped the Superb and approached the gate. At least he could get directions as to his whereabouts. What he wanted now was a drink, a meal and a bed, in that order. To his surprise the gate was locked; he shook it fiercely, but he was no Samson, so thoughtfully he returned to the Superb. Whoever was inside wasn't taking any chances. A few yards further on he came on the second gate, and now his luck seemed to have changed, for when he attacked this postern—and no other word seemed so suitable —it swung under his hand, and he went marching up the semi-circular drive like the advance of the Valkyries. On the ground floor the shutters were closed, and very wise, too. It was the sort of night no one could want to admit. A naughty night to swim in, he thought vaguely, dredging up the quotation from the ragbag of memories he called his mind.

He pressed the bell and could hear the sound ringing through the house. Even if no one felt inclined to open the door, he was no stranger to a conversation carried on from a window. But whoever was inside was in no mind to make his acquaintance. Even when he thundered on the knocker there was no response. It occurred to him that the light might be a blind, which would account for its being so faint. People leaving their houses empty sometimes left a light switched on; some of them augmented the effect by leaving a radio playing. Only surely no one hereabouts anticipated burglars. He stood there for some minutes, alternately ringing and knocking without anything happening. The light burned with the same faint resolution as before. There wasn't an animal on the premises, or it would have come barking and whining at him. Sadly he turned and trudged back the way he had come. All the same, he didn't believe a house of that size and type—it might have been an old rectory, he thought, which pre-supposed a church reasonably near, and where there's a church there are people—would be wholly deserted. Quite soon he felt the Superb bumping over a cattle grid and then he was out on something that had some right to call itself a road. There was even a bus stop that might give him some idea where he was.

The first thing he saw chalked on a fence near by was BULL in huge white letters, but either some hopeful farmer had set up the notice with the idea of preserving his field from campers or the bull had the good sense to go away for the weekend. There was no notice on the bus stop, which was a Request sign only, but just beyond he found a bridge, and when he had crossed that, he came to the church. That church looked the most closed place he had ever beheld: there was the ubiquitous iron gate, firmly padlocked; there was a woebegone notice fastened to a dripping tree, the ink run in the rain. The notice said there would be a service next Sunday at nine A.M., but there was nothing to show how long it had been there or which Sunday was implied. He moved cautiously up the lane running alongside, but the only sign of life was a ruined house where workmen were either demolishing or rebuilding some unspecific erection. A short way further on, a wooden fingerpost said Dora's Field, pointing drunkenly to the left. Footpath only. All he could see beyond that was the side of a black hill.

He stamped back to the main road, and as he did so he saw a belated bus coming in the opposite direction. His heart accelerated, since buses have to come from somewhere, they don't spring up out of the earth—and the most probable place is a town. There might still be time for the drink, the meal, even the bed if he hurried. Back once more to the Superb and on, on. At the corner he slowed in case of opposing traffic, and doing so, chanced to look over his shoulder. The big house stood out a blacker botch against a world of shadows. It looked different now—it took him nearly half a minute to realize that the light that had been burning had gone out.

The landlord of the Poets Rest swabbed down the counter and exchanged a gloomy word or two with the only two customers in the bar. The beer they sipped was as muddy as the night.

"Quiet!" offered one, and "It's all this telly," mourned the landlord. "Ruination to the trade. Chaps come in for a drop to be consumed off the premises, and then it's back to the missus and the box. Don't know what's come over husbands these days. No spirit."

He was startled when the door was suddenly bounced open and a man, looking rather like Mr. Edward Bear, was catapulted in. He had the reddest hair and eyebrows Samuel Parr had ever seen, and his suit was an excruciating shade of brown; he wore a checked brown and fawn cap and he had feet like a catamaran. Considering the paucity of the custom, you might have expected the landlord to be pleased to see him, but he showed no such emotion. His slow mind registered the fact that this was a stranger, and they were prejudiced against strangers in these parts.

"Drink, food and a bed," invited Mr. Crook. "Evening, all. Nice to meet you. I was beginning to think I'd driven off the rim of the world."

There are some voices you take to at once, but so far as the landlord was concerned this wasn't one of them. "We don't do beds," he said in a sort of menacing bloodhound voice. "This isn't a hotel."

"You could have fooled me," murmured Crook. "Next thing I suppose you'll be telling me it's a temperance house."

Reluctantly the landlord measured him a pint. Mr. Crook swallowed it in the manner common to him with his first. He just opened his mouth and let the pint pour down. The three men watched him with interest. Mr. Crook set the glass down; he felt as though he'd been bathing in the Sea of Slops.

"Cheese?" he inquired when he'd got his breath back. "Ham? Bit of pie? Come on, you're registered as a licensed victualer, aren't you, and I'm certainly a traveler. And this is the only port of call I've struck in a dog's age."

"Ah, you won't find any hotels open, not to casual custom, not this time of year," observed Mr. Parr with satisfaction. "Out of season, see?"

"I'm Father Christmas getting my bearings," offered Mr. Crook. "How about a nice reindeer steak?"

A voice, sepulchral as that of a sexton, spoke from the shadowy bar. "Don't have the pie," it said.

Mr. Crook came back sunnily with "What's yours?" and both men answered at once. Crook said he thought he'd take some rum. "Whose is the big house by the cattle grid?" he asked.

"That belongs to old Mrs. Nick," said the man who had warned him against the pie. "Away just now, though, gone to stay with her niece at Broadwater for the winter."

"Then she's left her ghost behind," said Crook. "Wantoning and having itself a ball," he elaborated.

The landlord spoke apathetically. "Gentleman's got the wrong house."

"You bet your!" said Crook. "Gentleman's got the only house." He looked at the three faces shadowy in the poor light of the bar. It even occurred to him that on one of her numerous skids the Superb had overturned and he'd been so busy considering his next move he hadn't noticed he'd broken his neck. If this is the next world, he reflected, we're deceiving a lot of innocent little children.

The third man, who hadn't spoken up till now, said in a voice as heavy as suet duff, "Gone to stay with this niece, like Amos said. My girl, she helped her pack."

"Then she's unpacked since. When was she supposed to go?"

"Tuesday," said the man who wasn't Amos.

"And I'll tell you something else," continued Crook. "You want to wake up from that nice sleep of yours. After I'd stood hallooing at the gate for about a quarter of an hour and had gone my hopeful way, someone put out the light."

"Trick of the moonlight," said Samuel Parr. "Stands to reason there's no one there."

"If you can see a glimpse of a moon I'm the Astronomer Royal," retorted Mr. Crook in his extravagant way. "There was someone there all right, and I'll tell you something else. That someone was still there when I moved on. You could hear anything in that Valley of the Dead on a night like this. Listen to it." Automatically they all inclined their ears in the direction of the door. "Wind dropped, not a footstep, not a cry. Stands to reason anyone there must have come by car, so why didn't I hear it starting up? No, your old lady changed her mind —it's always happening. You're talking to the man who's forgotten more about the sex than most chaps ever know."

It said a good deal for his powers of persuasion that none of the three attempted to contradict him, they didn't even look skeptical. When providence blows something like Mr. Crook across your path you don't argue, you simply accept.

"Not much worth taking there," offered Samuel Parr at last. "Lives on the smell of an oilrag by all accounts. Great rooms with dark red paper and bookcases right up the wall, photographs going back to the Ark, but according to my wife she's been wearing the same hat for four years and she got that at the local jumble."

"Sounds like my cup of tea," said Mr. Crook wistfully. "Who lives with her?"

"There's a companion, old Mrs. Fisher, she goes in most days, but no one else actually lives there. Had a little dog for years—Sandy that was."

"Name or color?" speculated Mr. Crook.

"It was more a biscuit really, got very old, snappish, had to be put down at last. She wouldn't have another, said it wasn't fair when she couldn't exercise it."

The door of the bar opened again, and a man wearing a police constable's uniform came in. "Here's Mr. Doyle," said Parr in a pontificating way. "Gentleman thinks there's someone in the Poets House, Joseph."

"Shouldn't be," said Mr. Doyle. "Old Mrs. Nick was due to leave Tuesday. Hired Tom Benson's car, going to stay with her niece at Broadwater, same as last year."

"Anyone see her go?" inquired the skeptical Mr. Crook.

Mr. Doyle considered. "There's Tom Benson. Always hires Tom's car when she goes away. Rector was at her—why not try that new garage by the Clock Tower—well, they don't ferry goats in them. But no! I'm used to Mr. Benson, she says."

"Funny an old lady living out there all by herself," Crook persisted. Of course, they did it all the time in London, but London was different, London wasn't a great black wilderness full of unidentifiable birds—sparrows he knew, and robins, and he might have been able to identify a blackbird, but the black-backed gulls, the kestrels, hawks, crows and the occasional night-

haunting owl that he had encountered during his few days' so-
journ in the district were all as strange to him as something out
of an Arthur Rackham illustration. "Any folk—except this niece?"

"There was a son, got himself killed in a climbing accident—
oh, twenty years ago—old Mr. Nicholas died a year later, and
there was never a grandchild. Young Stephen got killed before he
got wed."

"Big place for one old lady," Crook urged again, and saw they
were regarding him with a look of pitying sympathy. It wasn't a
look he was used to, and he wondered why.

"That's what her niece says," conceded P. C. Doyle. "Why don't
you live in a hotel, there's some nice hotels hereabouts if you
want to stay in the neighborhood. Meet nice people there."

"Maybe she don't fancy nice people," suggested Mr. Crook
intelligently.

"Of course Mrs. Glass, that's the niece, married to a doctor,
they come from a town, and townsfolk don't understand. Like
sheep I think they are sometimes . . ."

"Why knock sheep?" murmured Mr. Crook. "A lot of chaps
hereabouts must get a living out of them."

They went on talking as though he didn't exist.

"Like to huddle together," Doyle said. "But with us" (he meant
country folk) "it's different. I tell you" (and here he did turn
politely in Crook's direction) "there are old women, seventy-five,
eighty, living in cottages on the hillsides where they could be
dead a week and no one know."

"Milkman?" suggested the urban Mr. Crook.

Doyle shook his head. "They don't do deliveries, not just to
isolated houses. Well, you couldn't expect it. Two miles off a road
some of them are."

"And then they say the race of martyrs is dead. You mean the
old girls fetch their own." By this time it would hardly have
surprised him to learn that the cows called in person to be indi-
vidually milked.

"Mrs. Nick she does have hers delivered," Doyle allowed. He
had just come off duty, but he gave the impression he was ready
to stand considering the situation for the rest of the night. "But
some of these isolated homesteads" (Crook liked that phrase)

❧

"there's old Miss Ainger, she goes down to the Leather Bottle, still has one of these metal cans with a lid. Mrs. Rouse is a farmer as well as running the inn, well, her son, Jim, mostly does that, but she'd have milk for outlying cottages, give you a nice cabbage, garden stuff, some of the carriers leave their parcels there, well, it stands to reason they can't go climbing hills and fording brooks—there's Mrs. Banks, she has a water-splash . . . you have to swim that more or less in bad weather . . ."

"Who's Mrs. Banks?" asked Crook, feeling a bit dazed. "A duck?"

"Gentleman's from town?" suggested Doyle. There was no scorn in his voice, but it carried a note of commiseration.

Crook answered like one cock calling from a steeple to a rival cock in the next village. "Coziest little place you know. Name of London," he agreed.

"London," repeated Doyle simply, as if no other comment were necessary. Crook would have agreed that it wasn't.

"You don't have to believe everything they tell you," he assured Doyle. "Now in London we believe in being neighborly; even if some do call it nosey it comes to the same thing in the end."

"I drop by when I can," Doyle went on with a steadfastness the Last Minstrel might have envied. "The whisper goes round—So-and-So wasn't at the W.V.S. bazaar, that's Friday mornings, well, more a market really, opens nine o'clock, queue waiting a full quarter of an hour before the gates open, stalls cleared of every-thing worth having before ten. Not seen at the Oxfam Coffee morning, and she wouldn't miss that—social occasion, see, as well as a good cause. So someone goes round—sometimes me. I tell you, sir, there's times I'm half afraid to ring the bell."

"Not your fault," objected Mr. Crook.

"Ah!" said Doyle, nodding his big bullet head. "Now that's something you don't get in London, I daresay. Sense of responsi-bility. You're right, of course, if anyone should break in and do these old ladies, well, even a policeman can't be in six places at once, but I represent the law hereabouts and the law should be where the evildoers abound. Not that we get a lot of crime, mostly kids and tourists getting a bit wild. I'll look in on Mrs. Nicky in the morning, and thank you for mentioning it."

❈

Mr. Crook turned, and to his amazement he found that during this interchange a plateful of cut bread, butter and cheese had been placed on the counter.

"If you fancy a bit of pickle," offered Sam in his mournful voice.

"It wouldn't run to a bed, I suppose?" Crook sounded hopeful, but you can't win them all.

Samuel Parr shook his head. "There's only the attic and Sally's there. She's expecting any minute—my missus has been with her half the day."

"First litter, isn't it?" contributed Doyle sympathetically. "That's when they need a bit of encouragement. Well, of course, if Sally's on the bed the gentleman couldn't very well disturb her. I wonder now—could I have the use of your telephone, Mr. Parr?"

His use of the landlord's surname told everyone he wanted it for official business.

"At your service, Mr. Doyle," returned Sam formally.

"I might be able to help you out," Doyle explained to Crook. "We're not London, of course, but we don't like to disoblige strangers."

He went to the telephone. Mr. Crook ordered rum all round. The silent man accepted his with a bow, then observed to no one in particular, "Benson was to Wainwright's Tuesday afternoon."

"Wainwright?" repeated Sam. "Why didn't you tell Mr. Doyle?"

"I wasn't to know he was meant to be taking the old lady to Broadwater, was I, now? Three o'clock this was."

"And she was to go eleven-thirty—that's what Tom was saying to my niece. Post comes late these mornings, late as eleven sometimes."

So, of course, Mrs. Nick had waited for the post.

"She'd take her dinner at the Frisky Lamp at Aldwater, the way she always does when she goes away," speculated Sam. "Meet old Mrs. Fisher, I expect, though I did hear Mandy Fisher's been took bad these last few days. She was asking for one of Sally's kittens," he added in parentheses, "but now—I don't know. Reach Broadwater say half-three. Half an hour for a cup of tea, home by six, say." He shook his head. "Couldn't be done, Jacob. Not if it was Tom Benson in Wainwright's."

"It was Tom all right."

The door clicked as the policeman returned.

"My brother-in-law, Fred Ferris, could fix you up for the night," he told Crook. "Any friend of Mrs. Nicky . . ."

"Haven't the honor," mumbled Crook, who was beginning to feel like one of those great weeds that grow under the river surface and are swept inexorably to and fro by the moving tide. It made him feel slightly dizzy.

"You brought us the news about the house," Doyle explained. "We think a lot of Mrs. Nicky hereabouts."

"Give the lady a tinkle?" Crook suggested, but not particularly hopefully. He had the idea that Messrs. Doyle and Parr would as soon suggest ringing up Queen Victoria.

"Where did you say this light was, sir? Upstairs?"

"That's right. Don't you have electricity hereabouts? This looked more like a candle . . ."

He'd touched on a sore subject. Not only did they generate their own electricity, their lakes were being robbed to bring electricity to the neighboring manufacturing towns.

"If she didn't want her neighbors to know she was still in residence . . ."

Crook burst into a howl of protest. "This is 1967, not 1867, when by all accounts ladies drew down their front blinds and sat at the back of the house to let the snobs think they were taking the waters or whatever in a foreign spa." He pronounced the word as though it ended with a capital R. "If she didn't go after all, as arranged . . ."

"*That man,*" said Mr. Doyle impressively, "has a deal of power, I daresay, but he still can't make laws to tell folk when they can leave their own houses."

"I wouldn't be too sure," retorted Mr. Crook recklessly. "Never surprise me to hear they passed a bill this very afternoon . . . Oh, well." He seemed slightly surprised to see that the bread and cheese had all disappeared. "Did I eat that?" He pulled out some money and paid his scot. "Where does this brother-in-law of yours hang out?"

Mr. Doyle gave him directions. As he turned away the landlord put on the radio. It was the mixture as before—the familiar names reeled out: Vietnam, the Common Market, the Freeze, work stoppages, news of the latest war-threatened zone—nothing to the effect that Arthur Crook, the well-known eccentric lawyer and criminologist, was visiting the north of England and was about to stir up yet another antheap, but at the end something did come over that held all their attention. A young man called Frank Piper, who had got away from the notorious Cumberton Prison a couple of days previously, was now believed to have escaped from the prison area and had been reported traveling north, in the direction of Carlisle.

"Wonderfully mobile, these escaped prisoners," was Mr. Crook's hearty comment. "I bet he's been seen in Cheltenham, Cardiff and John O'Groats. What was he in for?" Because it hadn't been a local crime and he hadn't been asked to intervene, and he liked to assure all and sundry he didn't stick his nose in where it wasn't wanted.

"Broke into a house and helped himself to some notes he found lying around," Parr said. "And when the old gentleman came in unexpected-like he crowned him with a brass candlestick."

"It was a pitiful case," put in Doyle unexpectedly, and Crook was startled by his choice of an adjective. "Young chap's wife was sick, there was a little girl, about two she'd be then, Piper took French leave to look after them, and his foreman turned unreasonable. They had words and Piper was given his cards. Faults on both sides, I daresay, but the next thing was the young fellow got behind with his rent, got into more trouble with the Labour because he wouldn't take a job outside the district, they threatened to cut off his unemployment pay. Even if they took the wife into hospital, there was still the little girl."

"Landlady not the maternal type?" Crook offered.

" 'Put her into care,' she said."

"And Piper got notice to quit?"

"That's about the size of it," Doyle agreed. "Well, like Mr. Parr told you, Piper went out, found this house open and seemingly empty, saw the money on the desk and was helping himself when the owner came in and tried to call the police."

"And got himself knocked out for his pains. For the count?"

"Well, it didn't improve his beauty," Doyle allowed in his sedate way. "Mind you, Piper didn't help himself much. Old fellow was rolling, he told the court, what was twenty quid to him? It was my home to me. The magistrate made a big thing about a hulking young coward attacking a defenseless old man, and Piper told him he'd seen machines on the workshop floor looked more human. Does he think you can live in a tree in mid-March? he said. Well, he got three years, lucky not to be charged with grievous bodily harm, they told him, but he'd not been in trouble before. State kept the wife and child till Mrs. Piper was able to go out to work—if he'd behaved himself he'd have been out in a few months, only it seems the little girl kept asking for her daddy, why's Daddy gone away, doesn't Daddy love us any more, you know how kids are."

"Bachelor myself," said Mr. Crook in dignified tones, "but I'll take your word. Can't have the sense he was born with, must realize the rozzers have only got to plant a man outside the wife's door . . ."

"He doesn't expect to show a clean pair of heels," Doyle assured him. "Just wants to see the little girl, explain about working south, back soon—there's something wrong with the law, Mr. Crook . . ."

"You're telling me," agreed Crook heartily. "Trouble is, they don't listen to chaps like us when we try to thump a bit of common into their blocks . . ."

"Should be something like they have in the army, compassionate leave. If they'd let young Piper back it's my belief he wouldn't have given them any trouble, but a man's a father before he's a citizen. As it is, I wouldn't like to be the man tried to stop him seeing the child, not if he's as near as they make out. He'll lose his remission, of course, country'll be keeping him for the full term and a bit over if he gets into more trouble while he's on the loose, the way they mostly do. Well, he has to eat, hasn't he? Doesn't make sense, really."

"Some of these prison Johnnies don't deserve their criminals," Crook agreed enthusiastically. "The way they mislay 'em!"

"I'm not a legal gentleman," Doyle pursued (at that stage it hadn't occurred to any of them that Crook could by any power of imagination be so described), "but you know what they say about the looker-on. A man's only got one life . . ."

The light had faded altogether from the sky as Crook hopped back into the Superb, and already a spatter of rain blew through the menacing tree trunks. Lucky if he didn't lose his way again, he thought, a shade despondently. It was stretching the arm of coincidence too far to suppose he might, earlier, have been within a stone's throw of the missing man. This old Mrs. Whosit must be crazier than a coon not to have got into a civilized environment before the winter storms began—true, it was near spring by the calendar, but they seemed to run a calendar of their own in these parts.

Poor old trout, he hoped she was tucked up nice and cozy in her niece's guest room, whatever the locals might believe to the contrary, and knowing nothing of the intruder. Even he couldn't guess that old Mrs. Nick had done with civilization, as generally comprehended, for good and all.

ii ❖❖

IN HER COMFORTABLE modern house in Broad-
water Mrs. Doreen Glass looked up as her husband came in with
the morning mail. "Anything from Aunt Abby?" she inquired.

"Give her a chance," said Dr. Glass. "She probably doesn't feel
like writing letters, not if she's a bit off color. If it was anything
serious you'd have heard from that doctor feller."

"I don't know why he couldn't have sent us a message in any
case," grumbled Doreen. "Aunt Abby's an old lady . . ."

"An old witch," amended Gerald Glass. "I'd like to see anyone
doing something she didn't approve. No coward soul is mine,
but if your aunt forbade me to get in touch with my kith-and-kin
you wouldn't catch me risking my immortal soul defying her."

"Why should she—not want to keep in touch, I mean?" Doreen
demanded. "I must say he was pretty cagey on the phone—not to
worry, but probably just as well for her not to travel for a day
or two, everything under control."

"What more do you expect the poor chap to say? What really
staggers me is that she had the good sense to call in a doctor at
all. Are we having any tea this morning or is the pot just for
ornament?"

"That's my point, she wouldn't have called him in for something slight." Carelessly Doreen swept some tea out of the pot,
partly into the cup, partly over the tray.

"Then perhaps she didn't want to come," suggested Gerald
Glass. "After all, at seventy-five she must have earned the right to
change her mind if she wants to."

"She's got the telephone, it wouldn't hurt her to use that."

"When she's ready I don't doubt she will," said the doctor. "My

17

oath, you don't know when you're well off. Most of these women can't keep off the phone . . ."

"He was pretty careful not to say exactly what was wrong. You don't think she could be . . ." she hesitated, then touched her forehead. "She's always been a bit on the eccentric side."

"In that case," retorted her husband heartily, "I wish there were a few more like her."

"Living out of the world like that . . ."

"Not out of her world, only out of yours. Which she'd probably describe as a lunatic asylum, all this to-ing and fro-ing . . . Anyway, an eccentric, as you call 'em, wouldn't be very noticeable up there, they get 'em all shapes and sizes."

"And I'd had the guest room done up especially for her," mourned Doreen, "with that lovely rose paper, just to please her."

"It beats me why you should expect a gardener to enjoy seeing roses grow up a bedroom wall, no roots, no pruning, no watering, nothing. Agin nature, I'd have said. Not that it wasn't a kind thought," he added hurriedly (until that moment he'd hardly realized the room had been redecorated, but he knew his wife's taste in wallpaper). "You'll see, as soon as she's fit to travel she'll be down."

"I even offered to go up and fetch her," Doreen pursued. "I don't like the thought of her being alone in that dreary mausoleum . . ."

"It's not a dreary mausoleum to her, it's her home. And we don't know that she is alone. There's that Mrs. Stork, Mrs. Heron . . ."

"Mrs. Fisher."

"That's the one. Now do stop fashing about your Aunt Abby, Doreen. She's got along pretty well for seventy-five years and it hasn't all been gravy—losing that boy of hers, a lot of women would have gone to pieces—and being married to a man twenty years her senior, like Arnold Nicholas, must have been rather like sleeping with someone off a Crusader's tomb, beats me how he managed to give her a son—no, all things considered I'm not surprised if she prefers her own roof when she isn't feeling up to snuff. Why, even snails . . ."

"It's a good thing you only operate on the National Health," Doreen burst out. "Private patients do like their doctors to behave like normal people. Snails indeed!"

"God has been good to the snail!" quoted her husband. "It has a coat of mail. And a house in which it can travel night and day. Which is more than most of us can say."

"Snails get their armor, if that's what you call it, cracked by thrushes for breakfast, and the toughest nuts break if someone steps on them. Can't you see, you ape, I'm worried over her?"

"That comes of living in an urban area. Up there, those great landscapes, they make a man and his troubles seem pretty small beer. Now, wait another twenty-four hours, and you'll probably get a message. If not, you can ring her, can't you?"

"And get her out of bed if she happens to be alone in the house? You know the telephone's in the hall, and she won't have an extension in her room."

"Well, she's got this doctor, if he thinks it's necessary he'll go round, and remember, no news is good news. And don't suggest ringing up now, because its practically surgery time and . . ."

"I have an intuition," said Doreen unhappily.

"Another? It's a good thing these intuitions of yours can't take physical shape, the house 'ud be overrun with them, a rabbit warren wouldn't be in it, and there's no myxomatosis for female instincts."

"I'd ring him," Doreen pursued feverishly, "but he didn't give me his name. Doesn't that strike you as odd?"

"Perhaps he had an intuition, too, and perhaps he wants his phone for his regular patients. Anyway, why shouldn't he be her own doctor?"

"She hasn't spoken to a doctor, according to herself, in twenty years. I don't suppose she's on anyone's list."

"Well, perhaps he's got her into a hospital." Dr. Glass looked at the watch on his wrist. "The first of my anacondas will be here any minute, and I haven't even had a second cup of tea." He pushed his cup across the table.

"There's as much likelihood of anyone getting Aunt Abby into a hospital as of getting her into a beauty parlor, and you know it."

Her husband pushed back his chair. "Have a good time in your Chamber of Horrors," he said heartlessly. "At least you don't have to pay entertainment tax on it."

He swallowed his tea and made for the door. He talked a lot of sense most of the time, a knowledgeable chap, and not really without heart, but the best of us can get caught short and this, as his wife was going to remind him interminably in days to come, was about to be his Day of Reckoning.

At about the same time as this conversation was taking place, P. C. Doyle mounted his bicycle, a machine in its way as honorable and remarkable as Mr. Crook's famous Superb, and almost as immortal, and set out on his morning round. Everyone he passed knew him and gave him a greeting. Pausing at Tom Benson's machine shop he looked in to find Tom out but Mrs. Benson in charge.

"It's not like Mrs. Nick," said Mrs. Benson. "Very considerate as a rule, but of course anyone can be taken bad."

"Like that, was it?" said Doyle. "Must have been bad to cancel . . ."

"Well, it was the doctor," said Mrs. Benson. "The one the niece married. Said they'd been a bit bothered, she didn't sound like herself, so he'd come up in his own car to take her to Broadwater."

"Didn't call in on the way?" Doyle suggested. "She'd pass the door."

"Well, you know how it is with these city folk, Mr. Doyle, too much of a hurry to give you good morning. Mind you, I did tell Tom he should charge something, I mean, he turned down another client for Mrs. Nick, but you know Tom. Not that she won't send something," she added more generously. "A very fair-minded woman, Mrs. Nick. If that niece doesn't stop her, that is. That one's so near she'd be standing on your feet before you knew it." She moved her head uneasily, like an animal scenting bad weather. "There's nothing wrong, is there, Mr. Doyle?"

"Not so far as I know," Doyle assured her. "It's just that I heard Tom was to Wainwright's Tuesday afternoon, so it stands to reason he couldn't be taking Mrs. Nick to Broadwater. Funny she didn't leave her key at the station the way she always does when she closes the house."

He came away feeling uneasy. Nature has her own way of doing things that is respected by country folk. It's when things happen out of the ordinary that you start looking for squalls. He got back on his cycle and pedaled in the direction of the Poets House. Last night's storm had blown out completely; the sky was a clear pale blue. Some cattle in a field turned lazily inquiring heads as he passed. The ground was marshy enough, but the stream under the bridge Crook had crossed the night before flowed brilliant and cool. There was a cormorant sitting on a low branch waiting for a fish. All life is there, thought P. C. Doyle. Mad Maggie came swinging and lurching down the road, accompanied by a little dog of anonymous parentage; it wasn't much larger than a fur flea, and most of the time it ran on three legs. Maggie boasted it could go twenty miles, but when it had been put to that test was anyone's guess. She grinned at the policeman, baring enormous prominent teeth. On impulse he stopped to say, "Going to see Mrs. Nick, Maggie?" and she shook her wild head so that her hair flew out from under its gypsy-patterned scarf, and she swung her hands and laughed uproariously. Then all of a sudden she was somber. "She'm gone," she said in mysterious tones.

"Gone to stay with her niece at Broadwater," Doyle agreed.

"She'll not come back," prophesied Maggie.

"Now, come, Maggie, you know Mrs. Nick wouldn't desert her own place. It's just for the bad weather."

"Houses don't like being left alone," Maggie told him. "No, Mr. Doyle, she'll not be back."

"Time will show," returned Doyle pacifically. He cycled on. No one paid any attention to what Mad Maggie said, but there had been an authentic ring in her voice that was somehow chilling. The road was bad here, he couldn't make much pace. The Poets House looked empty enough this morning—shutters at the lower windows, upper sashes fastened, both gates closed, not a glimmer of light to be seen. He even started to ask himself if that chap from London could be wrong—it didn't occur to him Crook might be playing a practical joke. Even at a first meeting you could tell he wasn't that sort of a man. The gate through which "that man" had claimed to pass was locked all right today, but then, as Doyle knew, it had an automatic action. Whoever had been on the premises the night before must have appreciated that and fastened back the catch. P. C. Doyle went down on his haunches and examined it. As a young lad he'd been in and out of trouble like a wireworm through a three-prong fork, though never anything serious, mischievous really, full of curiosity and devilment; there weren't many even now could teach him much about getting onto premises where he'd no right to be. When they heard he was putting in for the police there'd been a gasp locally. They'll never take him was the general opinion, but to everyone's amazement he passed the test.

"We can do with a bit of spirit," remarked the officer who interviewed him. "And then he's not the ambitious type, always thinking about getting his stripes. The place where he was born will suit him."

He had a quality for which this officer couldn't find the actual words—sympathy maybe; what it amounted to was he liked people, especially his own people.

"He'll be a good copper," this man reported to his superiors. "He's never been in any real trouble, not even in front of the juvenile court. He's the sort of village officer our kind of folk appreciate."

He had shown considerable perspicacity. P. C. Doyle fitted into the landscape like a tree or a rook on its nest. You don't really notice it, but if it disappeared something in the landscape would be missing. He never agitated to get into the plain-clothes branch, he liked his uniform, and he contrived so that it never created a barrier between himself and his neighbors, and yet retained its own respect. He married a nice sensible woman, had one son who was as different from him as chalk from cheese, joining the army when he was eighteen and now breezing around the world at his country's expense. Not so different from his old man really, Crook would have said. They both liked to see a bit of life, but they liked to see it in different places and at a different tempo.

Now on this bright spring morning P. C. Doyle came somewhat ponderously to his feet. Since the gate was now locked it followed

that whoever had been in the house at the time of Crook's visita-
tion had now left, closing the gate behind him. He recalled that
the old lady kept a spare key under a flowerpot outside the
garage door for emergencies. Most of the inhabitants of these
solitary houses did the same. The garage was built back from the
house down a gravel slope, and this door also was locked. Not
that anyone was likely to try to steal her blunt-nosed ancient
Arethusa, which looked as though it had crawled out of a swamp
in the Dark Ages. It was known all over the county, and the old
lady still drove it herself to attend local functions from christen-
ings to burials. Fifty years she'd been driving and never had so
much as an endorsement; and if she did now and again park in a
prohibited area there wasn't a police officer in the district who
was going to give her a ticket.

He noticed some crushed marsh marigold petals on the ground
in front of the garage door. Only one place they could have come
from, and that was a lush valley in the woods known as Marigold
Bottom. There wasn't really a motoring road through that part of
the woods, but if Mrs. Nick had taken some old lady home last
night, as might well happen, she could bring the car through a
gap in the trees through the bottom and so on to the road known
as Falcon Lane, though it was only a secondary road at best and
had an evil reputation after dark. Even lorry drivers often
avoided it, making the detour through Rosebery. At one time it
had been the rendezvous of a gang who if they wouldn't actually
hold up a lorry would attack a solitary motorist, to say nothing of
a pedestrian, simply for kicks. Still, a thing like that wouldn't
prevent Mrs. Nick taking her own path, and Doyle wasn't sure his
sympathy in those circumstances wouldn't be with the attackers.
She possessed a good earthy sense of justice that didn't square
with some of the modern mewling ways.

Anyone tried to hold her up, she'd be through them like a knife
through butter, the policeman reflected. It's always a mistake to
assume that good people have to be fools or soft.

It's not right, Doyle continued reflecting. If the old lady hadn't
been fit enough to make the journey to Broadwater on Tuesday,
what was she doing tooling about in her car in Marigold Bottom
on, say, the previous night? He moved uneasily to where a row of

flowerpots stood alongside the garage. He found the key he wanted under the fourth flowerpot, and stood for a moment weighing it in his hand. Before he could come to a definite conclusion as to his next act he heard a fresh step, and looking up, saw a dark little man wearing heavily pebbled glasses that still failed to conceal very bright dark eyes. This was Jimmy the Post —someone had so dubbed him years ago and for some reason the name had stuck.

"You're never delivering here," exclaimed P. C. Doyle. "Didn't Mrs. Nick fill out her usual form for having her letters posted on?"

"Not that that gives us much to do," Jimmy agreed. "Never much of a one with a pen, that one. But seemingly she didn't go, leastways not to the niece." He held up a garishly colored postcard very carefully and economically penned. "You get to know handwriting over the years," he explained blandly.

"And in particular when it's a card." Doyle looked at it thoughtfully. "I never knew any woman to get more on a postcard than Mrs. Glass. But why should she be writing here?"

"Because Mrs. Nick never went to Broadwater; she postponed herself at the last minute, from what I can gather . . ."

"Mrs. Benson was telling me Tom had a message from the doctor—Dr. Glass that 'ud be—that he'd come up special to fetch her." Doyle struck large purposeful hands together. "I knew there was something wrong, Jimmy, the minute that London chap started to tell us about the light. Lights don't switch themselves on and off in empty houses." They stood staring at each other, two homely, troubled men.

"I suppose her car's still in the garridge," offered Jimmy at last, but more really for something to say than because he expected this to supply an answer to their problem.

"That's something we could learn," Doyle agreed. He fitted the big old-fashioned key into the lock and pulled open the grumbling wooden green door, swollen with years of rain and pitiless weather and thundering upland wind. The old black Arethusa was there all right, and on the garage floor were more of the golden petals, trodden and mud-stained. Doyle took a step forward.

"Pity machines can't talk," offered Jimmy. His wandering gaze went over the hill; his eyes, sharp behind those disfiguring glasses, picked out a hovering heron like a shaft of light. A lovely bird, he thought . . .

His attention was abruptly recalled by an indescribable sound emanating, he realized with a shock, from P. C. Doyle. For a minute he was utterly confused by the stranger at his side. The stranger opened a big unfamiliar mouth; his cheeks seemed discolored, like the cheeks of a dead man.

"Someone," said the unrecognizable voice, "is going to swing for this."

Because Doreen Glass's hunch had paid off, for once, Mrs. Nick's luck had run out at last, and it wouldn't matter how many postcards she wrote or telephone calls she made, no one was going to be able to tell her niece just what it was that had prevented her from making the familiar journey to Broadwater two days before. At least that's how it seemed at that stage when practically no one in that part of the world had connected the outrage with the name of Arthur Crook.

While time seemed to come to a standstill, Doyle stood staring at the car and the unrecognizable hunched creature huddled into the driving seat, a crushed blue felt hat jammed over her bony forehead, a bruise on her temple and a face that told anyone as knowledgeable as the village bobby the official cause of death. Not a nice death, not the sort of death an old lady looks for that's been respected for years and given respect in return. There was no need to touch the icy shriveled hand or the cold leathern cheek. A doctor might be able to put a period to the time of death, the fact would be obvious to a child.

Jimmy peered under the taller man's lifted arm. "Christ!" he whispered. He caught Doyle by the wrist, led him out of the shed and into the open air; but when he saw his face he uttered a sharp involuntary cry. "No, Joseph," he exclaimed, "you may be the law but that doesn't mean you can take it into your own hands. This is a job for the C.I.D."

P. C. Doyle drew the breath into his lungs as though it would suffocate him. "They can have it," he said at last. He'd never envied the plain-clothes branch, the death-and-glory boys. It might be their pictures got into the papers, but they didn't belong to a community the way the chaps in uniform did. Now he walked past Jimmy as if he didn't see him. And perhaps he didn't. His vision was infested by an old head with a discolored face, skin drawn tight over the bone, tilted back and that livid purple bruise above the eyes.

"Knocked her out," he said at last in a voice as wooden as the old tree beside the gate. "Jammed her into the driving seat, turned on the exhaust, the way you wouldn't put down a dog. Must have hung around till it was finished, though." He pushed back and found the old woman's big shabby black bag on the passenger seat. Pulling on a pair of gloves he opened it. "As I thought, she didn't need the emergency, opened the door with the one she carried."

"It's not likely to be the chap the gentleman from London found here," Jimmy offered. The story was all around the place already, of course. "I mean, it's not to be supposed he'd hang around—and it was Monday Tom's car was canceled."

Doyle looked at him as if he thought he wasn't talking sense, or if he was, it was irrelevant. His voice had the heavy anguish of a man who seldom loses control, but when he does, look out for the holocaust. Heaven send whoever it is is a good few miles away by now, Jimmy reflected. Doyle in this mood was unpredictable. A good copper, they didn't come better, and just, too, knowing that A (though a villain) has the same rights under the law as B (the lawgiver himself), that all that matters are facts and that the rain falleth on the just and on the unjust alike. Mercy is for every man, Jimmy recalled, but let Joseph get his hand on the one who could be concerned in the death of an old woman, and this old woman in particular, and justice is going to fly out of the window faster than the atom bomb.

Doyle spoke again. "Jimmy, you stay here," he said. "I'm going along to the box at the crossroads and ring the station, then I'll be back. But you can't leave her alone, not now." He remounted his cycle and rode away. He asked for Detective Chief Inspector Mount and was told he was out, so reluctantly he made his report to an inferior. He delivered the truth with a brutal and brief simplicity. Such questions as what the hell P. C. Doyle was doing investigating a crime on his own account and technically breaking into someone else's garage could stand over. He took his instructions—go back and hold the fort, don't touch a thing, you'll be relieved the first possible minute—with a grunt of acquiescence. He agreed with Crook that mouths are made to shut as well as open, but he did a bit of thinking on his own account, and before he returned to the Poets House and the brief vigil before the high-toned plain-clothes cars came roaring up, he had put out a big cautious hand and dialed another number, this time that of his brother-in-law's house.

It was Fred himself who took the call. Yes, he said, the gentleman was still here, yes, he'd pass the message along. When he got the drift of it Doyle heard a sharp intake of breath, then Fred agreed he'd daresay that inspector 'ud want a word with Mr. Crook, "and if a word's all he gets he'll be lucky," he wound up. "Got a nose for the job, I'd say, and noways nesh with his speech."

Saying which, he rang off.

iii

INQUIRIES WERE WELL under way, though nothing of importance had been turned up, when the four men met at the Golden Goose at midday.

"Of course, now the plain-clothes branch has taken over, you could say the matter was out of our hands," Doyle agreed, lifting the tankard Mr. Crook had thoughtfully ordered in advance. "It's my belief that one of these days they'll be getting computers to solve every manner of crime, and then we'll all be redundant."

"And they'll succeed when computers commit them," Crook agreed heartily. "Not before."

"It beats me what's the sense of all these machines if they're only going to do the same as men only more so," interposed Fred candidly. "But what Joseph means, Mr. Crook, is that in a thing like this it's not just what happened that counts, but why, and that's what you can't expect this city lot to understand. Oh, they're as bright as new sixpences"—he paused, drawing a deep breath—"funny to think we won't have any more of those if this government gets its way—but it stands to reason all they'll have to go on is facts, and you can't get motives out of facts."

"And that's the truest one of all," agreed Crook soberly.

"Mind you, if there had been something" (some reason to make Mrs. Nick go in fear of her life, he meant) "it's not likely she'd have talked. She'd had her troubles, my da remembered her as a girl of sixteen keeping house for the doctor—he was a widower when she was fourteen—working like a carthorse, out over the Fells day and night when most of the houses hadn't got telephones and you did a lot of your traveling on horseback. There wasn't all this interference in those days," he added wistfully.

29

"Everyone wondered what she'd do when the old man died—she wasn't above nineteen or twenty—there didn't seem any family for her to turn to, and then she married this old fellow more than twenty years older, her da's friend he'd been, a geologist they called him. Used to give lectures at the local workingmen's club; I went to one, I mind, interesting it was, all about the Ice Age. There's a valley here called the Valley of the Skull . . ."

"They do like their names twopence colored, don't they?" murmured Crook respectfully, signing to the barman to recharge the tankards. Not that he had any objection, he liked everything a bit larger than life. And the whole setup fascinated him, it was like taking an immense step backward in time—these huge skies and yawning valleys after the bright narrow streets and the flaring lights and the cosmopolitan company of Earls Court and the Bayswater Road. Variety is the spice of life, and spice was what he looked for wherever he went.

"Split right across," Fred continued. "You go down, down, and then you start the climb on the far side. Steep as a precipice and the cliff at the top cut like a face—the Duke's Head it was called, strangers used to think it was an inn. We had a rector once, always using that in his sermons as an example of the good life— down into the valley of the shadow and up into the sun."

"Out with your seven-league boots and step over?" offered Crook hopefully. "Or didn't they go for that kind of sense?"

Doyle grinned involuntarily. "It's a pity you couldn't have met our rector, Mr. Crook. Well," he took up his brother-in-law's story as neatly as an actor coming in on his cue, "Mrs. Nick getting married the way she did surprised everyone, though it was agreed she couldn't be expected to go and live in a town, like putting a wild bird in a cage. She went about a lot with her husband at first, then after ten years we heard she was expecting. That was a surprise, if you like, you wouldn't have thought Mr. Nicholas had enough humanity in him to give her a child. More at home with a geologist's hammer in his bed by all accounts than a woman. Still, Mrs. Nick being what she was, there was never any question in anybody's mind who the boy's father might be, and funny thing was he was the spitting image of his da. Young Stephen brought a lot of life into that house, too bad he got himself killed in a climbing accident when he was twenty-five. Even then she never said much. Old Mr. Nicholas died a year or two after that, but she stayed on in the big house by herself. No grandchildren, see, but I doubt it crossed her mind to move. It's a funny thing, no one ever seems to have thought of her as a young woman, but even after she was gone into the seventies you couldn't think of her as old. There was something there, it's like a bit of ground behind my cottage, always green, because there's a secret spring underground somewhere, and even the developers who'd run us dry for their own benefit if they got the chance can't touch that. She was the same, always a green shoot, hat green with age, and her face with that weather-beaten look you find in old women who garden and go around in open cars, but something fresh—I wouldn't know the right words."

"You're doing all right," Crook assured him.

"Yes," Doyle discovered. "You'd understand, Mr. Crook. There's something of the same about you."

"I take that very handsome." Crook beamed.

Which brought them back full circle to their original problem —why should anyone wish evil to so harmless an old woman?

"Only two reasons," offered Mr. Crook. Either she had something X wanted and she wouldn't part with, or she knew something she mustn't be allowed to tell. "From what I've gathered, she don't seem to have had a pile of diamonds stashed away or a bundle of notes under the floor or even a map of hidden treasure in the attic, so—what did she know? And, even more to the point, how long had she known it?"

"When we know the answer to that one we'll be halfway home," opined Doyle solemnly. He hadn't been idle; he knew that Mrs. Nick had attended a meeting of the local Lakeside Poets' Association on the night of her death, had spoken of traveling to see her niece the following day, and no one had remarked anything unusual about her.

"So if she changed her plans it could be it wasn't her own choice," Crook reflected. "Maybe what she knew was something she only learned that night."

But all this speculation took place before they found the second body.

The official police force was going great guns. Mount, an ambitious and fussy individual, had never had charge of a murder case before, and what was the black death to an old woman and a source of outrage to a whole country community represented an immense opportunity to him. An imposing array of "lads" drove up to the Poets House and took charge in a manner that would have made old Mrs. Nick turn in her grave if there had been time to plant her there. But at the date of their arrival in shining modern police cars she was in Mr. Pinnock's Funeral Parlor—another source of fury to those who had loved her and who considered that the right place for a corpse was the house where its spirit had lived for fifty years. Still, it was agreed, she wouldn't want that nosey lot prowling around, and at least Mr. Pinnock could ensure privacy.

Inside the house were more traces of trodden marigold petals and clods of damp earth, but insufficient evidence of identity in the sense that there was nothing so definitive as a clear footprint. Still, scraps of marsh grass and some of the tiny pebbles from the stream where the flowers grew convinced the authorities that they were on the right track. When they came out of the house the inquirers were surprised to see how many people had collected—cameras snapped, questions were asked, even the press seemed to be blowing it up into something considerable.

"It's undignified," said P. C. Doyle, "that's what it is. It's my belief if they got the chance some of these vultures 'ud take their cameras right inside the death chamber."

Mrs. Nick's old black leather handbag contained a shabby wallet with a few pound notes in it and some documents of identification—driving license, membership cards of various ancient monument societies and literary associations, two blank checks for emergencies. The latchkey was in a zipper pocket. Inside the house half the rooms had been closed, presumably for years. The immense drawing room overlooking the lake, where meetings had been held in old Mr. Nicholas's day, and his book-lined study, the paper still dark red and patched with damp, his card-index untouched since his death, still had a waiting air, as if his ghost might come tramping through the hall and take up residence. The only lived-in room on the ground floor was a sitting room whose walls were covered with photographs, daguererotypes and a number of enlargements from amateur plates, and furnished with good old-fashioned pieces, china, silver—a period piece of the kind Arthur Crook would appreciate. On the high mantelpiece were cards of invitation to functions she couldn't have attended in any case, a confirmatory note from Tom Benson as to the time he'd collect her on the Tuesday and a rather garish picture of parakeets from Doreen saying she was expected and her visit pleasurably anticipated. The telephone instrument was in the hall, with a small personal directory beside it, and her suitcases, all except the overnight case which was discovered upstairs, were neatly locked and arranged by the front door. Everything in order, you might say, for departure. And what a departure there had been, though not the kind anyone had anticipated. In spite of the fact that everybody knew she'd gone, and gone for good, the house still had an air of occupation. Even that cold-blooded mollusk, Mount, would hardly have been surprised if a dominant old voice had called down the stairway or a door had clanged on a landing where no one ought to be. It was that air of normality that made the truth more shocking than usual. Because whatever this tranquil background portended it hadn't been murder.

At the bank the police learned that the old lady had called in person to draw fifty pounds in notes on the morning of the day she died. She had explained that she was going to stay with her niece, and liked to have some cash available. She brought in a few pieces of silver to be placed in the bank's strong room, as she did whenever she went away. "No jewelry?" the police officer inquired, and was told, "She didn't possess any except what she wore."

That was something else to be borne in mind. No attempt had been made to rob the body, though she wore a diamond ring, good stones in an ancient setting, and a diamond brooch shaped like a crescent that was worth three figures even to a fence. So it didn't look as though robbery was the prime motive. On the other hand, about forty of the fifty pound notes were missing, and it seemed unlikely that she had drawn the money and spent it right away. "If she was going out that night the odds are she wouldn't take the whole amount with her," officialdom decided.

So where had she put it? In a suitcase? In a desk? a drawer? There was no sign of the money anywhere. They even examined the furniture on the chance of there being a secret cavity in one of the tables, but those who knew her best could have told them that Abigail Nicholas would have had no use for that kind of flummery.

She appeared, in fact, to have been a singularly unsentimental woman. The only photographs in her bedroom—and that was a period piece, if you like, high bed with a honeycomb quilt and a wardrobe big enough for a passage if you knocked out both ends—were two of the dead son, Stephen, one a snapshot taken of him as a schoolboy, the other a studio portrait possibly for his twenty-first birthday. Stuck into the frame of the last was a curling picture of a black labrador and a small faded snapshot of a terrier—possibly the departed Sandy. No trace of a husband, not even a picture of old Dr. Adams. So far as could be seen no one had paid much attention to this room, but of course the criminal presumably had sufficient sense to wear gloves. Still, everything lay as Amos's niece had left it, neat and tidy, and as plain as the proverbial pikestaff. It was a different matter when they opened the door of the room Stephen Nicholas had occupied during his short career. Here a cupboard door swung wide, clothes had been torn carelessly from hangers and flung on the covered bed, drawers gaped, pairs of shoes had been separated and lay about on the rug. Until now the room probably hadn't undergone much change since the young fellow's death, even the window was left open a few inches, as though, like Peter Pan, he might suddenly come flying home.

"Someone wanting a change of gear," observed Mount superfluously. "Someone who knew his description had been circulated and had to change his appearance. So where does that get us?"

For his money, and that of a good many other people, come to that, all the indications pointed to Frankie Piper. It was too bad that no one could tell him just what clothes were missing, but the boy had been dead for twenty years and fashions change . . . Ann Piper had come north after the trial and sentence, he remembered; probably found it easier to get work where she wasn't so easily recognized. The police had called at the house but she had told them she knew nothing about the escape, had had no letter, no warning. 1458988

"He won't come here," she insisted. "He'll know you'll be hanging around." But they kept a watch on the house just the same.

Another reason for supposing the intruder to have been pretty desperate was the condition of the kitchen. The white scrubbed table was scattered with opened tins, the edges jagged and torn; there were crumbs on the floor, dishes in the sink.

"A lady like Mrs. Nicholas wouldn't go off and leave a place in that state," everyone said. The main question was: how did the interloper get into the house?—since it was established there had been no break from outside. The obvious answer was that he'd been brought in by the old lady herself, or admitted by her, though no one to whom Mount spoke could suggest anyone who might wish her harm.

"These old biddies, they haven't the sense they were born with," Mount commented irritably. "Not even a chain on the door, and so far from civilization she could scream herself hoarse and no one would hear."

"If it was a neighbor, someone she knew . . ." the sergeant suggested.

"A neighbor who'd suddenly developed homicidal tendencies, is that what you had in mind? There's no sense to a crime like this . . ." But of course there's sense of a kind behind every murder, even if the criminal is a homicidal lunatic. Suppose she'd been persuaded to give some passer-by a lift and he'd knocked her out—why? For the sake of the car? But the car was in the garage. For what she had? But her jewelry and handbag hadn't been pillaged, and how had X known about the other forty pounds? It wasn't the kind of thing you'd tell a stranger. Or someone coming to the house and asking to use the phone—a break-down car, an accident, someone hurt—difficult to refuse, and from all accounts the old woman had a sturdy sense of her own powers.

"If it was Piper," ruminated Mount, knowing all the same the danger of riding in front of the hounds, "she could have recognized him. What next? Perhaps she tried to call us—only why not just tear out the telephone, he'd have plenty of time to blow."

And then there was the fact that she was still wearing her hat and had been found in the garage. Nothing added up. And that London fellow who couldn't be persuaded to say he'd seen the light on Monday night, when the crime had taken place . . .

The last person who admitted to seeing Mrs. Nick living was an intrepid spinster called Jewell, who had one of those solitary cottages deplored by P. C. Doyle. She was one of the few loners who didn't drive a car, but that never prevented her getting around. There was nearly always someone to offer a lift, and if not, she demanded belligerently, what were feet for? On the night in question it had been Mrs. Nick who brought her home. Both old women had attended what was still, in 1967, described as a levee at Wintringham House, a sort of headquarters for the local Poets Association. They had left at about nine o'clock, the normal hour when such meetings broke up.

"That's when the witches' covens get going," Crook said when he heard, and he lifted his eyes as if it wouldn't surprise him to see a flock of ancient beldames on their broomsticks sweep through the cloudy sky. And quite likely it wouldn't. The meeting over, Mrs. Nick had confirmed her plans for the morrow; no one noticed anything unusual about her. It was understood that when she had deposited Miss Jewell she would take the short cut through the woods, which would bring her out near Marigold Bottom.

"It's not really a motor track," Miss Jewell acknowledged. "More for boys on bicycles, though you don't see many of those nowadays, but it was the way she always took. She said she avoided the main road and the night lorries which start coming through on the upper road about that time."

"It can't have done her car much good," suggested the police officer, but Miss Jewell tossed her intrepid old head and said casually that Abigail's car did what its owner demanded of it. "She used to say it was like her, made to last."

But when pressed to try and remember anything unusual she surprised her companion by hesitating.

"She said one thing that didn't seem quite in character," she acknowledged, "though I didn't think much about it at the time. Just as she was going she said, 'I wish I wasn't going tomorrow, I have a feeling that if I leave the Poets House now I shan't see it again.' And she turned and put her hand on mine, which was most unusual, she was the least demonstrative of women, and said, 'Pray for a short winter.' I remember," the old woman continued painfully, "I said, 'Look out for the escaped convict, they say he's been seen coming this way.' Why did I say it? I don't know. I suppose we'd been talking about him earlier in the evening. Naturally, I never dreamed she might meet him."

"We don't know that she did," the police officer told her shortly. "She didn't speak of her health, I suppose—mention seeing a doctor?"

Miss Jewell stared. "Why on earth should she see a doctor? She hadn't any use for them."

Mount had already done some of his homework.

"We know her niece had a message from a doctor explaining that Mrs. Nicholas wouldn't be coming on the Tuesday as arranged," he pointed out.

"We don't know anything of the kind," contradicted Miss Jewell flatly. "We know someone rang up and said he was a doctor, that's no proof. I could say I was a doctor . . ." And indeed she had one of those deep mannish voices that can easily give a false impression, particularly on the telephone.

Asked whether Mrs. Nick would give a stranger a lift late at night, Miss Jewell said it all depended—on the reason given, on the person offering the reason, on whether she recognized any such person.

"You think it could be someone whom she knew, then?"

"I don't see Abby giving a lift to a stranger, she had too much sense. But it doesn't matter how much sense you have if you don't have choice as well. And that's what we don't know, isn't it?"

But in that case why make the return journey? Why not leave the body in the wood? The case bristled with questions, to which at the moment no answers were forthcoming. Because the murderer had been privy to her plans, had canceled the car and rung the niece, it followed it was either someone who knew her or someone in whom she had confided, and it didn't square with anyone's knowledge of Abigail Nicholas that she should open her heart to a stranger.

The police, who seldom found themselves in accord with Mr. Crook, were at one with him in one conclusion, which was that (since it's improbable for an old woman of seventy-five to make a deadly enemy overnight) something had happened, been discovered, suspected, perceived, after the break-up of the party and the arrival at the Poets House, which constituted such a danger to a second party that murder was the only solution. And this happening, whatever it might be, had presumably taken place during the brief journey from Miss Jewell's remote cottage to the Poets House—because none of the yellow petals had been found on the dead woman's shoes, which meant they must have been brought in by the murderer. Say the car got into trouble going through that narrow ungraceful road and she had stopped and espied someone and called for help. It had been a night of constant change, darkening skies and then suddenly a flood of silver light as the moon came swimming into a patch as clear as the day. And she was no fool. She might be old but her eyes were still sharp.

"We'll have to search the woods," Mount said. "The answer may be there."

It was an unenviable task. A young constable, surveying the expanse, much of it overgrown, boggy and tangled with enough natural impedimenta to constitute a number of near death traps, remarked gloomily, "This is a job for dogs, not men. You could be looking for a week . . ."

A sergeant, overhearing him, retorted grimly, "When you opted for this branch, didn't anyone warn you it was a dog's life?"

And in point of fact they hadn't been looking very long before they found the body of the girl.

untidily, like a parcel or an the Don't know yet that she was

iv ◇
◇

SHE HAD BEEN thrust untidily, like a parcel or an old mattress, under a clump of brambles and rampageous roots quite near the Bottom. She might have lain there for days without being found if they hadn't been looking for some clue to the old woman's murder. That was one point. The second was that this was no death by misadventure; she hadn't just tripped or collapsed with a heart attack or even taken a handful of sleeping pills. Someone had deliberately pushed her out of sight, having first suffocated her. Because that, according to the medical evidence, was how she had died. Someone had put a hand over her mouth, possibly to prevent her screaming and raising an alarm, and pushed back her head.

"Mind you," the doctor warned Mount, "he may not actually have had murder in mind, just exerted more pressure than he'd intended. She had the bones of a bird. Quite a young girl—seventeen, eighteen at most. No attempt at sexual interference, no signs of pregnancy." And, in fact, it was later shown that she was *virgo intacta*. "Could be she just got in someone's way."

Mount saw all that. The thing that bothered him and was going to bother a lot of other people was what she was doing in a place like that, anyway. The Bottom was some distance from any residential quarter; the nearest houses were the farms on the other side of the wood, and anyone local would know the folly of a girl hanging about in Falcon Lane after dark. She wasn't even a pretty girl or one of the spirited fascinating kind, just a rather thin pale face, bony features, hair straight and mouse-colored—one of nature's misfits. Even her clothes were wrong—a duffel coat, a drab brown beret, solid brogue shoes—not the sort of

39

outfit you'd choose to meet a friend of either sex. And then this place—even the crazies knew better than to choose this spot for a rendezvous.

"Mind you," added Mount, "we don't know yet that she was actually killed where she was found. She could have been brought here from a car or even a lorry. I know not many of the drivers come down this way at night, but you do get the occasional daredevil, or if a driver had picked up a girl he might go out of his way to avoid being seen." Because there had been some ugly scandals about picking up passengers and now most of the owners had laid an embargo on their drivers taking these risks. "Only," added Mount with a natural cruelty of which he was unaware, "a man would have to be hard up for company to take a chance for this particular girl."

There was nothing at that stage to identify her, though presumably she wouldn't have come out without a handbag or even a powder compact. The motive could even be the small sordid theft—there was a case of a schoolboy done to death a few months before for less than two pounds. Mount had the search renewed for a bag or case of any sort, but nothing was discovered. The murderer, if he had any sense, would remove the bag; goodness knows there were hiding places enough in the woods, where quite large-scale operations had been carried on during the war and where there was at least one rubbish place that according to local gossip stretched halfway to Australia. Or he could have taken it away with him and dumped it practically anywhere. One thing was certain, there hadn't been much of a struggle, there was no trace of hair or skin under her fingernails, only the most superficial bruising—you could say she hadn't put up any sort of a fight. Shocked out of sensibility, said Dr. Morton, and dispatched before she knew what was happening. Why? For the same reason as the old woman was murdered—because she was an inconvenient witness. No, of course I've no proof, proving cases like these isn't my job, we leave that to your side of the force.

The girl's body approximated to no one listed among young women reported missing, and her clothes were no help. They had come from a well-known chain store, and bore no label or distinguishing mark of any kind.

"A girl like that—someone will be inquiring," Mount said. "She's not the tramp type—run away from home, I daresay, doesn't like her stepmother . . ." Only in that case you'd expect her to have luggage. She wore no jewelry, though that wasn't actual proof that she had had nothing of value when she was detained and killed. Only it seemed improbable she would possess anything worth more than a pound or two.

"There's the Brasher Gang," surmised Mount thoughtfully. "They wouldn't make anything of shutting a girl's mouth. There was that old fellow they knocked off a bicycle and cut up with chains and he hadn't a fiver on him."

Still, it was a long guess. Herbie and Ted Brasher were both inside, and the other two were lying low. And still that wouldn't explain what the girl was doing in such a place late in the evening. Could have answered a wolf whistle, of course, and got more than she bargained for, but in that case you'd have expected more signs of struggle. Or have got a lift, not realizing that nothing is for free, in which case the odds were she hadn't been killed in the wood at all.

In his heart of hearts he thought the silly creature had only got what was coming to her. Of the two, the old woman was by far the more interesting, and it had yet to be proved that the two crimes were linked, but he had to hope they were, because, if not, so far as Abigail Nicholas was concerned, they were back at Square One.

The dead girl was identified twenty-four hours later. Her name was Freda Woods and she was the daughter of a deceased schoolmaster and a cheerful extrovert mother who had remarried about a year previously and was now expecting her second child. Her story was a sickeningly familiar one. Her parents' marriage had been a poor preparation for the future. Douglas Woods had been ambitious, neurotic, his own worst enemy.

"He never got the jobs he thought should come his way," the widow explained to the police. "He was frustrated, and poor

Freda took after him. I don't know what it was, they were both good people with a tremendous sense of duty, only that doesn't seem to be enough."

The fact was that both lacked the human impulse. Also, although even candid Dora didn't admit this, both believed Douglas had married beneath him, as they said. Dora's father was a farmer; Douglas was of university stock. After her father's death, when she was about fifteen, Freda withdrew more and more into herself. He had left them comparatively poorly off, and Dora went out to work as an assistant in a second-hand bookshop in Lamsville, run by a man with the improbable name of Bill Christmas. Twelve months later she told Freda she was getting married again.

Freda was horrified. "That man? You can't."

"I'm thirty-eight, love," her mother said. "I've a long road ahead of me, and I like walking in pairs."

"Doesn't Father mean anything to you? Not that you ever understood him."

"And then," Dora said in her simple way, "she found there was going to be a baby. I suppose children never think of their parents as real people."

"You're right there, Mrs. Christmas," agreed the officer who was taking her statement. "I've got two boys of my own—you'd think they'd been born by a computer to hear them go on."

"On Monday evening my husband and I went to a party his mother was giving for her birthday. When we got back it was fairly late and everything was dead quiet, so I thought she'd gone to bed and wouldn't want to be disturbed. It wasn't till next morning when I went to take her a cup of tea that I found the room hadn't been slept in and there was this note propped against the clock. I brought it with me."

She opened her bag and took out a folded piece of paper written in a rather scrawling uncharacteristic hand.

I've gone to London to stay with Aunt Olive. [That's my first husband's sister, Dora explained.] I may not be her ideal niece but I'm the only one she's got, and she can hardly refuse me a bed till I'm on my own feet. You don't have to worry about me,

I shall get a job, they say they're crying out for secretaries in London, and as soon as I have a permanent address I shall let you know. Don't think I'll come back, you've made your life and I've the right to make mine.

There was a postscript that threw unexpected light on the situation.

I have borrowed your pearls. You always said they were meant for me, anyway, and you needn't be afraid, I shall take great care of them. But just in case things don't work out I shall need something and I suppose they're worth about £100. If I have to pawn them I'll send you the ticket, so you won't be the loser. And if everything goes well, as I expect, I'll send them back by registered post right away.

"Had she ever done anything of this sort before?" the police officer inquired.

"Run away, you mean?"

"Borrowed valuables."

"She never needed to. If you're asking did she take money out of my purse, anything like that, no, never. The fact is, she was badly upset. She'd got this friend, a girl she met at the secretarial college, and got the idea they'd have a flat together in London. Well, I could have told her Rosamond Peirse wasn't that kind, she had the boys round her like flies. The fact is my girl was expecting to go out with Rosamond that evening, and Roz telephoned—something better had turned up—I think that's what tipped the balance. Poor girl!" she added, and the tears brimmed her warm brown eyes. "After Douglas went she got the feeling she didn't fit anywhere. Not that my husband—my second husband—is to blame, he did everything he could to make her feel at home, but you couldn't help her. I know, I tried. I suppose that was the last straw, she just lit out. Mind you, it never occurred to us there'd be anything wrong. She and her Aunt Olive never did hit it off, so we were ready for a London call the next day, only what came was a p.c. in the afternoon, stamped Iona. It appeared that my sister-in-law had set out with a friend on a cultural motor-coach trip. Naturally, that altered everything. We rang the South

Kensington flat, thinking the housekeeper might be in residence, but there was only a builder's man, they were having some redecorating done. We decided to wait one more day before we went to the police, we knew she'd never forgive us for the publicity—and you couldn't have expected anything like this." She pushed back her hair. "I haven't quite taken it in yet," she said. "Why should anyone want to do a thing like that to a girl like Freda? If it had been Roz, now—but . . ."

"There's the pearls. They've disappeared."

"And how would she have got there? She could have got a train to Bond Halt, there's a connection from there to London Road—she must have missed that and thought she'd walk. And even if she got a lift, though I can't see Freda taking one, why stop in the middle of a lane? I mean, it's not as if there was any sign of a fight . . ."

"You could give us a description of the necklace, Mrs. Christmas," the officer said, and she passed one weary hand over her face.

"There was nothing special about it," she told him. "I never could understand why they should be worth so much, why any jewels are worth so much. They weren't a particularly striking string, but the pearls were beautifully graduated and it had a rather nice rose diamond clasp. The insurance company who valued them might be more helpful." She supplied the company's name.

"Do you need my wife any longer?" asked Bill impatiently. "She shouldn't be standing about—this has been a fearful shock . . ." He was concerned not only for Dora but for the child. She had lost her first in tragic circumstances, he intended to safeguard the second at all costs. "About the inquest?" he added, but they told him it would only be a formal affair, closed almost as soon as it opened, just evidence of identity and cause of death, after which the funeral arrangements could be made. No need for Dora to attend . . . if and when further evidence was obtained the inquest would be reopened.

Dora stumbled to her feet, feeling as though she had been climbing a mountain. She had a comfortable squirrel figure at all times and now in the sixth month of her pregnancy she tired easily. Turning to leave the station, her eye fell on a poster that had been pinned among a number of others on a board on the wall. It represented a young man with a thrusting face and thick brushed-back dark hair. Underneath was his name and description: Frank Piper, aged twenty-seven, dark hair, dark eyes—and a request for assistance if he should be seen or even presumed to be seen in the neighborhood.

Dora stopped to stare. "That's him, isn't it?" she said. "The one you think may have killed my daughter."

"We don't know that he ever set eyes on Miss Woods," the officer explained. "Oh, there have been reports that he's been seen in the neighborhood, but similar reports have been coming in all over the country. They always do."

"Didn't I hear his wife was working in this part?" Dora pursued.

"About forty miles away."

"So the odds are he would be making for this county."

Her husband's hand on her arm urged her forward. "Come, love."

But she stood her ground. "If they did meet and she recognized him—his picture had been in the paper, we both saw it, she took after her father, a very strong sense of duty—she'd think it only right to tell the police . . ."

"Would he know that?"

"She'd tell him, I'm sure she would, or let him realize— My husband was the same, that's why he didn't always get the positions he thought his scholarship deserved. They both thought a great deal of duty. If the pearls had been left to her she'd have thought it right to give them or their equivalent to Oxfam, say, and she wouldn't even have had any sense of generosity. And if she uttered what he thought were threats and he heard someone coming and wanted to silence her . . ."

"We can't act on suppositions," the officer pointed out. "Yes, of course it could have happened like that, but so far we've no evidence at all. But we shall get it," he added firmly.

Dora shook her head. "It won't help my daughter now. All right, Bill, I'm coming." As she moved slowly toward the door the officer heard her say, "That's the worst part of it in a way, that no one could ever really help her, not since Douglas died, not her own mother or you or even Rosamond. It's all such a waste, to struggle for eighteen years and then die in the dark with nothing accomplished."

"Gives you the creeps, doesn't it?" the officer murmured. Police work was supposed to harden you in time; you thought of the victims as bank clerks think of bundles of notes, something impersonal, the stuff of daily employment, but Dora's face haunted him. It wasn't the girl but the mother who called forth his compassion. He looked up to see a young constable watching him, open-eyed.

"And what's the matter with you?" he demanded. "Got paralysis or something? Are those reports done?"

The young fellow bent hurriedly over his typewriter. "Coming up, Sarge." He banged at a key and three rose simultaneously and stuck. His sergeant watched him ironically as he strove to free them.

"Don't mind about the machine," he observed. "That's only government property."

The constable realized it was going to be one of those days when nothing went right. Who'd be a copper? he thought.

The police put out inquiries regarding the dead girl and appeals for assistance from anyone who might have seen her on that fatal Monday night. Her movements during the earlier part of the evening were not difficult to trace. She had taken the local train to the Halt, where she should have picked up the London connection, but thanks to a stoppage on the line this had departed before her arrival. Her frantic, rather haughty inquiries elicited the information that no further trains would be running that evening that could enable her to catch any London connection. But there was a night train from the London Road Halt.

"There'll be no bus running before morning," the ticket collector assured her, and she had thrown back her thin arrogant face and cried, "It's your responsibility surely. It's your train that was late, I've booked a ticket, I have a right to expect to be taken to my destination."

"What do you expect us to do?" the ticket collector had demanded.

"You must have a railway bus or something . . ."

"At this hour of the night?" said the collector. "You're joking. Look, don't you know anyone hereabouts?"

"I have to be in London tomorrow," insisted the girl.

There was a hint of hysteria about her manner now that made the man look at her more closely. "You traveling alone?" he demanded. "Don't you have any people?"

"I'm going to London to join them."

"You can't do it tonight, and you can't stay in the station because it's just about to close."

"I suppose there's a local garage or something where I could hire a car? It's urgent. I had this telegram . . ." she improvised.

He gave her the name of a garage where she could probably get a car to take her to the London Road Halt.

"You're all right for money, love?" he asked a bit uncomfortably, and she tilted her head even further back—a neck like a chicken she had, he told the police—and told him coldly that naturally she was. He saw her turn in the direction of the garage, and after that his hands were full seeing the last of the passengers off the premises and closing the station for the night.

"You didn't find out if she got the car?" he was asked, and he said no, he hadn't, it wasn't his job.

At the garage they knew nothing of her. It was clear she hadn't called, so obviously she had decided to walk to the Halt.

"Could she have done it in the time?" was the question. The answer seemed to be no.

The next witness was a Mrs. Lovibond, who kept a late-night café on the Main Road. She recalled a girl answering to Freda's description coming in to inquire the way to London Road Halt, saying she had to catch a train and wanted to know the shortest road.

"You can't do it tonight," Mrs. Lovibond had told her sharply. "Does your mother know . . . ?"

"You can leave my mother out of this," the girl had said.

"If you're thinking of catching the late train, you'll never make it," the woman warned her. "Anyway, this is no place for a girl of your age to be on her own this hour of the night. Oh, I don't say you couldn't get a lift, some of these drivers are up to anything, but— Why don't you ring your mum and ask if they can't come and fetch you?"

It didn't escape the notice of the police that at every turn the girl impressed people as being young and quite incapable of guarding her own interests.

She might have been eighteen, Mrs. Lovibond allowed, but you could see she had no more sense than a chicken just out of the egg. However, when the woman made her suggestion, she said fiercely, "I don't see why you should assume I'm alone. As a matter of fact, my friend is outside in a car, but we don't know the road, and it's very important I should get the train."

"So I told her about Falcon Lane being a short cut," Mrs. Lovibond acknowledged. "Mind you, if I'd guessed she was by herself— But there's always a certain amount of custom that time of night, there's not another café open between here and Hartsborough—" In short, she had given Freda directions and the girl had gone out. "Didn't even buy so much as a cup of tea," added Mrs. Lovibond. "Not more than a thank you and that grudging."

"You didn't hear a car start up?" the police inquired, and she shook her head.

"What I mean is, there were cars coming and going all the time, I wouldn't notice one in particular. She'd said she had a car—well."

"If she really was in a car at that stage it could only have been someone she'd just picked up," the police brooded. "Or someone who'd picked her up, more likely. So it wouldn't be a friend. And if it was a local chap, how come he didn't know the road?"

Stranger still—how was it that she had been found by Marigold Bottom, a place where no car would voluntarily stop? It wasn't a road that was much used at night anyway, thanks to its evil reputation and bad surface. And if anyone had been out on it on the fatal evening he was keeping his lip buttoned. Not that that proved anything. There might be a dozen reasons why a fellow didn't want to advertise his presence in the lane after dark to the authorities, and none of them connected with the dead girl. If she had been lying to Mrs. Lovibond, it was improbable that she would elect to walk on the wrong side of the hedge, where the ground was marshy and treacherous. If she had been tramping along the road you'd have expected more evidence from her shoes and stockings. The most likely bet was that in desperation she had accepted a lift, the driver had turned into the lane as being quieter and more private than the main road, he'd started exacting payment for his services, and in the ensuing shemozzle the girl had come to permanent grief. It was the sort of case the police loathed above most, because the assailant would be virtually impossible to identify. He could even have been a chap with a screw loose.

"She most likely was seen," remarked Inspector Mount to a colleague on the case, "only no one's going to put his head into a noose coming forward, if he's got a good reason for not wanting the police to trace his whereabouts that evening. It doesn't have to have anything to do with the girl."

Inquiries were still going on about Frankie Piper, on whom the police were now pinning most of their hopes. A man known to be on the run on his own will often try and pick up a companion, preferably a girl, because if you're looking for a single man you may be thereby deceived. It's an old trick and doesn't often throw much dust in the official eye, but criminals often don't realize this. Mrs. Lovibond's story about the girl having a male companion in a car made them consider the possibility of Frankie's having lifted a car—no great difficulty as any young thug can tell you—and stopping the first girl he could persuade to listen to him. It would be chancy, of course, with his picture around everywhere, but some chances you have to take. Then—say the girl had recognized him or say she'd started making trouble, there was a motive for you all right. They redoubled their inquiries about Frankie, who was still being seen in several counties at once. And then at last they got a break.

The police station at Luddendon received a telephone call from a man who didn't give his name but who said he had a short time before given a lift to a man answering to Frankie's description. He strengthened his case by adding that the fellow was carrying a zipper bag with S.N. painted on it. It was the bag really that had attracted his attention, that and the chap's clothes, which were what he called *trendy*.

"Carnaby Street, I suppose," he had said. "Looks pure mid-Victorian to me. Seemed in a bit of a state," he added.

"How long ago was this, sir?"

The informant said, vaguely, about half an hour. "He seemed in a hell of a hurry to get away," he added. "It could be because we'd just seen one of these photographs asking for the public's assistance. I made some joking remark about wondering what it must feel like, and—well, that was the first time I noticed the case and I remembered what I'd read. He tried to get out of the car, and I tried to stop him; he got violent and it seemed best to let him go and pass the word to you. He took the Luddendon turning . . ."

"On foot?"

"Well, he was when I saw him."

He wouldn't give his name, he said his firm didn't like his giving lifts, but this chap had hailed him, and sometimes you used your own judgment; anyway, there it was, he thought he was giving the authorities a leg up . . . And he slammed down the receiver.

"They're all alike, aren't they?" said the police officer grimly. "Don't want to be mixed up with trouble, don't want to soil their hands. Leave it to the police, what are they paid for? Ah well, shouldn't be long now. Where did that chap say he was phoning from?" He checked. An A.A. box on the Lorchester Road. And this chap's had a half-hour start, ought to be about halfway by now.

He sent out instructions to his crime squad.

"If that fellow knows what's good for him he'll come quietly," he said.

Only criminals, like most other people, hardly ever do.

To Frank Piper, moving like a chamois from one dangerous peak to another, the world had turned into Looking Glass Country since the sudden appearance of his picture in public places like post offices and in frames outside police stations. At first he hadn't believed it. Lots of chaps skipped jail and the authorities didn't plaster their photographs on walls, like the train robbers or hunted murderers. Ever since he made his desperate bid for freedom, lying low, taking chances, sometimes bold, sometimes timid, but never forsaking his resolve, he had anticipated the touch on the shoulder, the word in the ear, and so far he had eluded them all. It was difficult to decide which was the better policy, to march boldly into shops, cafés, use public transport, allow himself to be seen as a member of the shifting, hustling, unnoticing public, or go by sidelines, moving after dark, in the hope of escaping observation. Now that he was so near his objective—he had always known he was, as it were, on a short-wave connection, his wasn't one of the lasting breaks—he felt that if someone tried to stop him at half past the eleventh hour he would react with the same violence he had shown two years before. On that other occasion, when he had looked about him in a strange room, with an enemy threatening him, he had seen the little solid brass-headed candlestick, and swung it. He had been told repeatedly how fortunate he was that the chap hadn't been mortally injured and he hadn't had to stand his trial for murder; and no thanks to Frankie that he hadn't, there had been no thought of moderation in his mind that day . . .

Still plodding onward he came to a crossroads and hesitated. This part of the country was no man's land to him, and he couldn't afford to take a wrong turning now. The sound of a motor horn roused him from his thoughts. A pursy-looking chap, a commercial traveler possibly, was leaning out of the window of his car and asking him if he wanted a lift.

"I'm going to Lorchester," the man said.

Frankie, who had bought a cheap map of the neighborhood, recognized the name as that of a place that would advance him several miles on his journey. He looked at the speaker; he sounded as though he'd had a pretty good lunch, mainly liquid. "Well," said Frankie, "if you could let me out just before we get there . . ." and threw the little zipper bag that had belonged to a dead boy whose name he hadn't even known a week earlier into the car and stepped in after it.

His mind seethed with the idea of somehow getting control of the car and making straight for Bindley Cross, where Ann and his child were living in lodgings. Only it would be madness even to try. The chap might be a bit sozzled, but he was still probably capable of putting two and two together, and he must have seen some of those damned pictures along the road. Still, time now seemed to be the essence of the exercise, and if this man didn't recognize him, the next fellow he encountered might, and some risks have to be run. In any case, he couldn't reach Bindley Cross soon enough to see Ann. It was odd—he'd broken out for Vicky's sake but now Ann was his main objective, the one true unshakable thing in a transient and treacherous world.

By what seemed a curious trick of fate his companion started to talk about fox-hunting. This, he remarked, was fox-hunting country, he'd seen a pack in action. A pretty sight. Not that he was a hunting man himself, he added, at least not so far as foxes were concerned.

"They tell you Reynard enjoys the chase," he said in a rich winy voice, "but if that's so they're more sporting than I'd be. Though they do say a good many get away."

He's talking to keep himself awake, Frankie realized, as the car reeled unevenly around the corner, and lucky for everyone the road was empty. Accepting the lift didn't seem such a good idea now; Frankie hadn't come all this distance and insured an increase of sentence in order to end in a pile-up on a north country road.

"The lucky fox that gets away lives to be caught another day," he suggested drily. "He can't win." He had a sympathy for foxes, coursed hares, anything that had the odds against it, he wouldn't have thought possible a week ago.

"*Homo sapiens!*" said the driver with a suggestion of a hiccup. "That's his epitaph. He can't win. The grave gets him in the end."

"No sense hurrying the day," Frankie suggested, and a little later he offered to take the wheel. "You look tuckered up," he said.

"It's a hell of a job," said his companion, and Frankie said, "Sure, sure." He wondered if the chap would drop off, in which case he'd have no compunction in belting through to the border of Bindley Cross and ditching the car. It would be awkward if they were stopped for any reason and he was asked to produce a license, but, as his neighbor had remarked, you can't win, at least not all the time. And with this fellow at the wheel the accident would be a dead certainty, the operative word being dead. He stole a glance at his companion; the fellow seemed to be dropping off. The car ran well, his spirits rose, it was good to feel his hands on a steering wheel again . . .

The voice beside him broke into his thoughts. "We're not winning the Derby," said the voice, and now it had a more succulent note. "We might turn up here"—he indicated a leafy empty lane—"I've got a flask in my pocket."

"Not while I'm driving, thanks," said Frankie briefly. "Besides, I have to be on my way."

"Got a hot date, then?"

"I have to get to Luddendon," said Frankie, who had seen the name on a signpost and realized it would involve a break with his companion before they reached Lorchester.

"What's a nice boy like you doing on his owney-oh?" insinuated the voice, and a hand came out and caught his knee. "Come on, if you travel with me to Lorchester you won't regret it."

Frankie knew a sudden wave of the fury that had got him into his present deplorable situation. Lucky, really, he was driving and hadn't a hand to spare, he reflected. "Take your goddamn hand off my knee," he said. "I'm no gardener, and if I were, pansies wouldn't be my favorite flowers."

The man beside him flushed a deep and furious red. "If that's the way you feel," he said, "you can bloody well get out of my car."

"I bloody will," Frankie agreed, bringing her up so sharply the engine stalled. He was out almost before she'd stopped trembling. He reached over the back and picked up the zipper bag with its incriminating initials.

"What d'you have in that?" the man asked with a sneer.

"Change of underpants and a pair of socks," Frankie told him. "And they're not made of blue crepe de Chine either."

"Let's see your driving license," said the older man unexpectedly.

"I must have left it at home," Frankie told him.

"You mean you've been driving my car without—you could have lost me my job."

"Which one?" Frankie asked unpardonably.

"I could report you to the police, taking advantage of me, stopping my car . . ."

"You do that," Frankie advised him. "Maybe if you ask them nicely they'll give you a breathalizer test."

Swinging the canvas bag, he went off down a road to the right without even looking to see where it led. The traveler sat where he was for a minute or two, collecting his senses, such as they were, before shifting over into the driver's seat. He carried on a brief conversation with himself before he prepared to move on. The words he used were brief, too, mostly only four letters. But Frankie's gibe about the breathalizer test had gone home. Hang it all, he'd only offered the fellow a lift because he might offer to take the wheel.

"Must have been mad," he told himself. "Could have been anyone, might have attacked me, he had a desperate look. For all I know . . ." And suddenly he stopped dead. "My God!" he whispered. He looked up and down the long empty sunny road. Frankie was making tremendous strides, as if someone had just presented him with a pair of seven-league boots. Two swans from a local swannery came sailing by, and he thought what splendid birds they were in the air and how graceful on water, and yet so clumsy, almost ugly, on the land. "Never can tell," he said. He pulled a box of little cigars out of his pocket and lit one. When he had smoked it he put the car into gear and drove along fairly slowly, watching the road. When he reached an A.A. phone box he stopped the car and got out and rang up the Luddendon police.

V ❖
❖

CARS COMING INTO the Luddendon area were surprised and for the most part affronted at being stopped and questioned by the authorities. When it was obvious they hadn't got the wanted man on board, they were asked if they'd seen a hiker who resembled him or been hailed by one. But it was no dice for the police, which wasn't surprising, since Frankie had had no intention of going near Luddendon, and had turned off to make for Bindley Cross less than a mile from the spot where he and his host had parted brass rags. But they got him just the same on the outskirts of Bindley Cross. This proved to be a picture-postcard village, with a triangular green and an ancient church with a little stone steeple like a dunce's cap, and a squire's pew inside to separate the nobility from the peasants. Though anyone could have told you the church saw little enough of either, even on the Sabbath. There was a phone box on the village green and Frankie entered it and dialed the number Ann had given him. She and Vicky had rooms with some old geezer who sounded like the burden hung around the neck of the Old Man of the Sea, but Ann said he shouldn't worry, she liked the child, and in a lot of places they only had to see a youngster to tell you No Vacancies almost before you'd opened your mouth. He knew the house had a telephone and he hoped it might be Ann herself who answered his call, but the thin rigid voice at the other end of the line was one he'd never heard before.

"Mrs. Piper?" it demanded suspiciously. "Who wants her?"

He wanted to demand, "What's that to you?" but exercised the necessary restraint.

"Her brother," he said. "And it's urgent."

"If you're ringing about her husband," said the grating voice, "he's not here, and we don't want him, what's more."

"Do I speak to my sister?" Frankie demanded, and he heard the sound of the receiver being put down. And then Ann was on the line.

"Harry here," he said sharply before she could say more than hullo! "You all right? They've got photos of Frankie all over, you want to watch out."

In his mind's eye he could see the owner of the unpleasant voice lingering in the hall or on the threshold, hoping to catch a word or two, the way you sometimes could on a local phone.

"He's not come here," said Ann. "Where are you calling from, Harry?"

"I'm on the green. I was wondering . . ."

Ann broke in, her voice changed. "Quick, she's gone, but she'll probably be back any minute. Frankie, you must be crazy, everyone's out for you . . ."

"There's a caff here," said Frankie, "called the Copper Kettle. I'll wait for you there."

"I don't know." It was unlike Ann to be so indecisive. "I think they may be watching, I'd simply lead them straight to you."

"If they've got the dogs out they'll get the scent anyway," Frankie assured her. "How about Vick?"

"Mrs. Paine will keep an eye on her. Look out, she's coming back." Her voice changed again. "I can get a bus from the Harvesters and be with you in—oh, say, half an hour," she told him. "That'll still give you time to catch your train."

He wondered cynically, as he hung up, if the old woman was fooled. The utmost he could hope for now was a little extra time. They'd get him, of course, he'd never had any illusions about that, but he could have his brief hour with Ann first, then they'd go back to the house and they'd see the kid, and that would be that.

He put back the receiver and came out into the benevolent golden light. A few people were drifting in through the doors of the Copper Kettle, old girls whooping it up, he supposed, because even a toasted teacup cake and a drink from a different cup made a change from sitting in your own room with Pussy on your knee.

And from his place behind the big oak tree at the far end of the green, the law watched him go.

The scene, until Frankie erupted into it, had been one of idyllic peace. Sunlight lay over the grass like a patina of gold; in the churchyard the ancient tombstones leaned drunkenly or confidingly (according to your taste) toward one another, many so old that moss had obscured the original names and dates. A couple of young chaps went by on bicycles; an elderly woman walked a fat spaniel. The church clock chimed the hour. But P. C. Ormskirk was oblivious to all this tranquillity. A young man of immense ambition, he had been on the lookout ever since the rumor went around that the escaped convict—that was how he thought of him, never as a fellow man in trouble, an agitated father, a desperate husband—had been seen heading north. Now he was more, much more, than a man who'd slipped his chain, he was a dangerous criminal with, probably, a couple of murders on his hands. If Frankie had held up those hands, P. C. Ormskirk would hardly have been surprised to see them dripping with blood. Making his rapid way to the now deserted phone box, Ormskirk remembered the case of a special constable during World War Two who had had the extraordinary good luck to identify a man who'd killed a London woman and for whom a nation-wide search was being organized. He didn't recall the actual occasion himself, of course, he was too young, but his father had been a village policeman before him and as a boy he'd heard the story. "Never shut your eyes except when you're in bed," the older Ormskirk would pontificate, "and even there a wise man sleeps with one eye open." This man who'd recognized the killer had been a special constable, retired and brought out again because of the war, and he'd recognized his man in a phone booth. It was too bad really that he, Percy Ormskirk, couldn't act on his own responsibility, but they didn't trust constables with murderers, and a man with his way to make—there were times when he fancied himself as Chief Superintendent P. Ormskirk, it had a lovely ring—didn't fall foul of his superiors. He watched Frankie go through the doors of the Copper Kettle. Lucky, really, you could see so well even from inside the booth.

"You're sure?" demanded the station sergeant, with less respect than his junior considered his due.

"He's carrying a zipper bag with S.N. on it, and his photo's everywhere," said Ormskirk, trying not to sound injured. "I've been keeping my eyes open ever since . . ."

"Well, go on keeping them open," the sergeant interrupted. "Don't let him make a monkey of you unless you want to spend the rest of your days pounding a beat. And don't forget that houses have a back entrance as well as a front, and Piper's slipped through enough nets as it is. The odds are he was phoning his wife; if she turns up, just keep her under observation too. He might need money and she just might be bringing it. So—don't do anything but keep your eyes peeled, and if you don't want to die young, don't let this one get away."

"Sarky old sod!" reflected Percy Ormskirk, coming back to his vantage point by the oak tree. Probably wouldn't have recognized Frankie himself. He was right about the wife, though, she came as a bit of a shock even to a man who believed himself impervious to surprise. There had been pictures of her in the local press, of course, after the news of the jail break became public property, but they hadn't done her justice. He wondered that he hadn't noticed her before, but she worked at the local china factory along with scores and scores of others, and presumably spent most of her spare time with her kid. He watched her dip her fair shining head—her hair was tied back with a ribbon, not floating all over her face like most girls—under the low lintel of the café. One of these days, he reflected, it might be nice to come back from the day's work to find that beauty waiting at your fireside (it was a truism that the devil had all the best tunes, and it was the criminal types who seemed to take their pick of the birds); lovely legs she had, and moved like a wave of the sea. No open shame, no furtive loitering, looking about her this way and that, you might think she was actually proud of the fellow, but then everybody knew what natural actresses women were. He looked at his wrist watch and turned to stare down the road.

"Come on!" he adjured the invisible police car. "What are you doing? Pushing it?"

And then he saw it coming down the road. It stopped a short distance from the Copper Kettle and two plain-clothes chaps got out. He hoped when medals were being handed around he wouldn't be forgotten.

The cretonne-overalled waitress (and you'd be looking at a chicken a long time before you thought of her) had just brought a pot of tea and some cakes to the table in the corner when the door was pushed open and the police came in. Frankie recognized them at once. "They haven't wasted any time," he said.

"Don't want any trouble, do we?" suggested the older of the two, stopping beside their table.

In an instant Ann exemplified the cliché so beloved of Arthur Crook about the female of the species.

"Don't they have to produce their warrants?" she demanded. "How do we know . . ." When she was satisfied on that score, she turned to her husband. "Don't say a word, Frankie," she warned him. "Not till you've seen a lawyer."

"Your husband knows his rights," one of the plain-clothes men pointed out.

"No harm reminding him of them," flashed Ann.

"Funny thing," said Frankie, putting his hands in his pockets, "I seem to have mislaid mine on the way."

"Watch it!" warned the policeman sharply, and Frankie laughed.

"I don't carry a gun if that's what you have in mind. They don't issue them where I've been. Bad staff work, I know, but . . ."

"We can do without the jokes," the policeman told him.

"What's life without a sense of humor?" Frankie asked mildly.

"They have to give you a lawyer if you ask for one," insisted Ann.

"I had one like that before—remember?" Frankie reminded her. "And look what happened."

"That was different. Then you knew what you were being accused of."

"He's being taken back into custody as an escaped prisoner," said the senior of the two officers in a stony voice. "Of course, if he's able to help with any other inquiries we may be making . . ."

"Don't miss a trick, do they?" said Frankie in admiring tones.

"I'm coming with you," announced Ann. "Yes, of course I shall. Why should they have all the witnesses."

"They won't let you do that, missus," the policeman warned her bluntly.

"Don't you start telling my wife what she can and can't do," Frankie commanded. "I'm the one she's promised to honor and obey, and she won't come to the station because I say not. Got that, copper? No, love"—he turned to Ann and his voice changed; it was like hearing summer come back over a winter landscape—"there's Vick. Don't want her waking up and finding herself a sort of orphan. I didn't take any particular shine to that dragon I talked to."

"She'll be all right with Vicky," Ann assured him. "But remember I'll get you the best man there is. You've got as many rights as anyone else, and don't you forget it."

Frankie glanced indulgently at his captors. "The way women kid themselves!" he said. "Still, I daresay you're both married men, you don't need me to tell you. Drink your tea, love, I could do with another cup myself, and I don't know what they may lay on at the station."

When they brought him in he wasn't foolish enough to try and deny his identity, but it was about the only thing he didn't deny. He didn't wait, of course, for Ann's mythical lawyer, he knew there are some miracles the Lord Chief Justice can't hope to achieve.

"Changed your name pretty smartly, didn't you?" they said, indicating the initials on the zipper bag. "Or have you really been Sam Noggins all along?"

"You must introduce me to him sometime," said Frankie cordially. "If you'd think he'd like it, that is. Nice chap, is he? Bit of a joke me picking up his bag from a market stall."

"That's where you got it, is it? You'd remember the day, I expect?"

Frankie considered. "Tuesday?" he offered. "Or might it have been Wednesday? Funny how the days all seem to run together."

"Couldn't have been Monday, I suppose?" the police officer asked.

"I was out in a neck of the woods, miles from civilization, Monday, that I do recall. No, say Tuesday."

"Happen to remember where you got it?"

"I told you—a market stall."

"Even market stalls have to be in towns."

"That's right," agreed Frankie. "That's where it was, in a town."

"Don't remember the name, of course."

"How did you guess?"

"But you might recognize it again if you saw it?"

"You're joking, of course," said Frankie. "Me recognize one stall from a score of others!"

"Bought your change of gear at the same place perhaps?" he was asked; and Frankie looked down at his out-of-date suit and told them, "You don't buy luggage and clobber at the same stall. Chap who sold me these must have been robbing a museum. Go right back to the Stone Age, I wouldn't wonder."

"Next time you help yourself to another chap's wardrobe," they warned him, "it could be a good thing to remove the tailor's tab."

"Fancy me not thinking of that!" Frankie marveled. "That's the worst of stir, you do get out of touch."

The tab in the jacket he was wearing said Beauvais, Martindale, and it was easy to establish that Mr. Beauvais had sold the business more than fifteen years before, retired first from Martindale and five years later from this world, and the chap who bought it had carried on under his own name. Henderson, that was. So laugh that one off, Frankie was invited.

"I've given my sense of humor the rest of the day off," Frankie said. "Well, it didn't seem very welcome. What happens now? Do you call up old Whosit from his grave and ask him to identify the suit?"

"There are others in the Poets House he made, same measurements, same style. Seems reasonable they were all made for the same chap."

"What's this Poets House you're on about?"

"As if you didn't know. Made yourself at home there, didn't you?"

Frankie shrugged. "If you say so. Who are these poets you're on about, anyhow?"

"You'd have to ask Mr. Beauvais about them. Must have been a bit of a shock when that London chap came knocking on your front door."

"Interfering bastard!" said Frankie mildly.

He put up a good fight, but of course he never had a chance and he must have known it from the start. It wasn't just the clothes or the zipper bag, he was asked to explain how he came to have thirty-seven pounds in notes in his possession.

"No one ever tell you you get paid for work in prison nowadays?" he questioned.

"Not like that, lad, not unless you're operating an illegal racket. You wouldn't want us to think that, would you?"

The notes, of course, had come, like the clothes and the bag, from the Poets House.

"Robbing the dead!" said the inspector in disgusted tones.

"Best person to rob," retorted Frankie. "Stuff's no good to a dead man. Not," he added carefully, "that I knew it belonged to a cadaver. Still, leaving money around in an empty house—it's not right."

He fought them every step of the way, though he must have known it was just a waste of time and breath.

"Why did you do it?" the inspector asked him.

"Take the money? I thought you knew. I needed it."

"And the old lady wouldn't part?"

"I don't know anything about any old lady. You're not telling me the house was haunted."

"The old lady the money belonged to."

"She can't have wanted it much if she left it lying around in an unlocked drawer."

"Ah, but she wasn't expecting visitors."

"Is that what she told you?"

"She was beyond telling us anything when we found her."

"Get along!" said Frankie. "Well, I'll tell you one thing, wherever you found her it wasn't in that house. The place was as bare as a newborn baby, and the note on the gate—*Closed*—tell you the truth I thought at first it might be some sort of museum. And I didn't change my mind when I got inside."

"How did you get inside, by the way?"

Frankie stared. "How do you suppose? Through the door. Didn't find any windows broken, did you? Well, come on, what's the charge? Breaking and entering? You'd have to prove it, wouldn't you?"

"The gate would have been locked," said an officer heavily.

"Ah, but they'd forgotten to put the broken glass along the wall. And they must have been expecting me or someone, because there was the key nice and tidy under a stone at the back."

"Didn't strike you as odd, seeing the house was supposed to be closed?"

"The old girl could have left the key for a cleaner or something, I suppose," offered Frankie vaguely.

"So you did know it was an old girl?"

"Well, not then, only there were tatty old raincoats in the hall and a squashed sort of tweed hat, and galoshes no fellow could have worn. Not that these are much better . . ." He looked down at the clothes he was wearing. "These jeans . . ."

"They were called trousers in those days, it wasn't a beatnik world."

"You'd remember, of course."

The man colored a bit. "You're not doing yourself any good, Piper."

"That should suit you," offered Frankie urbanely.

"Sir!" The police constable who had been emptying the zipper bag uttered a sudden exclamation.

"What is it, Blake?"

"There's something—must have slipped down through the inner pocket." His big hand was rummaging inside the bag.

"Don't say he's going to produce a rabbit?" Frankie marveled, but for the first time his anxiety was naked on his face.

"Some rabbit!" said the constable. His hand emerged from the bag, and he opened his palm and showed his superior what lay in it. It was a string of pale almost white beads with a rather striking clasp.

"Blow me down," said Frankie, "if I hadn't forgotten them. I meant to give them to Ann. How did I forget? Of course, you chaps came barging in."

"Don't forget you've been cautioned," said the inspector sharply. "You don't have to make any statement unless you wish to, but a lot of people are going to be interested to know what you're doing with those."

"I told you, I was taking them along to my wife. I bought a present for the kid from a five-and-ten store, and . . ."

"You're telling us you bought these there, too?"

"Any reason why I shouldn't?" Frankie asked.

"You'll have to introduce me to that store," the man told him. "My wife might like a string like that. Policemen's wives don't get many chances of peacocking round in pearls worth several hundred pounds."

"You gone nuts or something?" Frankie asked. "What's all this about several hundred pounds? That's just a string of beads . . ."

"That you picked up at a five-and-ten-cent store. I know. Only it's news to me, and it will be to the directors, that their sort of beads are issued with real diamonds in the fastener."

"You telling me those are diamonds? I don't have to believe you." But he looked really shaken for the first time.

"Shouldn't be difficult to establish. The lady the chain belongs to could identify it, I daresay, as well as her insurance company. They've been reported to us as missing, the pearls, I mean."

"Well," marveled Frankie, "what do you know?"

"Not as much as you, unless you choose to tell us. Still asking us to believe you bought it in a cheapjack store?"

Frankie shrugged. "All right," he said, "have it your own way, I found them."

"In the Poets House?"

"If they'd been there I wouldn't have thought they were just a string of beads, would I? Everything there was as old as the hills but it had class. No, I found them in the wood."

"Round the neck of a young lady?"

"If they'd been round the neck of a young lady I'd have known who they belonged to, wouldn't I? No, they were just lying in the grass. Just chance I saw them really. I'd been walking along the road—Falcon Lane they call it—and I could hear the traffic coming up behind me, and I didn't happen to want a lift, too many Nosey Parkers around anyhow, so I went through a gap in the hedge and I stopped by a sort of pond, well, more a big puddle really, I suppose, they must have had a lot of rain here lately. And some of the hotels I've been putting up on my travels, well, you'd be surprised, shocking service, not even hot and cold in the rooms, so I thought I might as well give my feet a bit of a rest and have a wash and brush up." (Crook was to say later, "If anyone tells you a damsilly story like that you must know it's true. A chimp would think up something more likely.") "It was rough, I know, but beggars can't be choosers and here were these beads lying in the long grass. First I thought, Someone's been having a bit of slap and tickle, only it seemed a funny place to choose, unless they were frogs, and I never heard of frogs wearing beads. I was going to leave 'em, and then I thought, A pity for them to be wasted, someone might as well have the benefit, why not Ann? Of course, if I'd known they were worth real money—if you're not screwing me, that is."

"We're not screwing you, and you're making this statement of your own free will."

"Why not?" said Frankie. "I'm the one that can give you the truth, and that's better than a copper's fairy tale. Well, I put 'em in my pocket. I work in a factory and it doesn't deal in diamonds. I never dreamed . . ."

"Didn't the girl tell you?"

"The girl?"

"The one who dropped them there."

"You can't have been listening. There wasn't anyone there, not even a lady frog."

"Funny," said the inspector. "Because that's where we found her, by the marigold plantation, tucked up nice and comfy under a bush."

"If she was playing games under a bush it's not my fault I didn't see her. And what's this about marigolds?"

"They didn't warn us you were color blind," the inspector said. "Marigolds are those gold flowers . . ."

"I didn't see any gold flowers. Maybe they were further on.

And if she was hiding among the flowers it's not surprising we didn't meet. What was she doing there anyway?"

"Well, she couldn't help herself, could she?" said the inspector with sudden harsh brutality. "She was dead, wasn't she?"

"Well, but I wasn't to know—wait a minute. According to the paper I saw, it was a Monday she left home with the necklace . . ."

"That's right."

"I wasn't anywhere near the place till Tuesday, so you see . . ."

"You told us just now you get your days all mixed up."

"I reckon Ann was right," said Frankie slowly. "I should have waited for that lawyer. Still, you've got your evidence, haven't you? That London chap—he said it was Tuesday . . ."

"When he came knocking on the door. What does that prove?"

"That it was Tuesday night I was there."

"Care to tell us where you were on Monday?"

"Holed up in a barn halfway up a hillside, hoping to God the farmer hadn't got a parental feeling for his blasted sheep and wouldn't come out and start counting them. And don't ask me where it was, because I hadn't got a map with me, and it would have been too dark to read it if I had."

"How did you get halfway up a hillside? Or did you borrow a bike?"

"I walked," said Frankie heavily. "It's what feet are for."

"Happen to meet anyone?"

"At that hour of the day—night, rather? Mind you, I was out early enough next morning, there are plenty of these young know-alls, call themselves climbers, climbers my arse. Up they come in their cars, start the hill halfway . . ."

"Ah, but it's the second half that counts," the inspector pointed out. "You come tumbling down from there and that's when you get your neck broken."

"Well, that's where I was anyway," said Frankie sullenly. "And if I'd known there were going to be all these questions I'd have left my visiting card. And I never saw any sheilah in the woods or out of it, dead or alive. It was just the way I told you—I saw these beads, I put them in my pocket, and after a bit I came out on to the main road again. There may be creatures that like living in bogs but I'm not one of them. I walked along for a bit, then I saw this road branching off, nice and dark, so I turned into that. And when I'd gone a bit of the way there was this big empty house . . ."

"How could you be so sure it was empty?"

"It was dark, wasn't it? And the gate was locked. Only there are ways of getting over a locked gate. Mind you, I knew whoever had gone hadn't been gone long, I mean, flowers out in the garden, no weeds . . . Then I found this key, and I got in, and I called out, but no one answered. I found a lamp—they live in the Dark Ages round here, don't they?—I lighted that and carried it round. No sense attracting attention. I wanted a change of gear and some food—I tell you my heart nearly stopped when I heard that chap tramping up the path. Tell you the truth, I thought it was one of your lot. Talk about policemen's feet. I thought he was never going, if I could have dropped a weight on his head— no sense of privacy. What did he want, by the way?"

"Lost his road," said the inspector.

"I don't blame him. Mind you, once his car was out of sight I scarpered. No time to straighten things . . ."

"We did notice that. By the way, this girl . . ."

"Which girl's that?"

"Oh come, Piper, you're not telling us there's more than one. Freda Woods, the girl we found under the bush . . . How was it? I suppose you didn't recognize your own strength . . ."

"You must think I'm stupid," said Frankie scornfully (and, of course, they did). "Do you suppose if I'd just killed a girl I'd hang on to a necklace worth—what did you say?—hundreds of pounds?"

"Ah, but you didn't know that, did you? Unless she told you."

"She didn't tell me because I didn't see her, but if I had, I daresay I'd have known she didn't buy it at Woolly's."

"How come? Did she look that posh?"

"I don't know how she looked, I didn't see her. Anyway, if I'd known they were hers I'd have got rid of them before now, wouldn't I?"

"Lots of chaps have thought that, but when it came to the crux they found it took more nerve than they possessed to chuck away something worth hundreds of pounds."

"You got cloth ears?" demanded Frankie rudely. "I tell you I didn't know they were worth anything, well, maybe ten bob or so. Mind you, I was crazy to think Ann would want some other girl's geegaws, but I hadn't seen her for a long time, and you like to take your wife something . . ."

"You could have dropped in at a five-and-ten on the way."

"And what would I use for money?"

"You had the thirty-seven pounds."

"Not then I hadn't. That was at the house. As if you didn't know!"

"It's too bad," said the inspector, "that you can't find anyone who remembers seeing you Monday night, I mean. No café bar proprietor, bus conductor, no chap you asked the time or borrowed a match . . ."

"Borrowed a match!" repeated Frankie scornfully. "That's a bloody silly thing to say. No, there's no one. I must have been wearing my invisible cloak. Still, it's up to you to prove I wasn't in the bar, isn't it?"

The news was on the radio that night and it made a nice bundle for the sensation mongers. The missing necklace had been found and identified by Dora Christmas as being her property, a statement that had been confirmed by the insurance company.

"I'd have been wearing it that night," Dora explained, "only the clasp was weak. I kept meaning to take it in to Mr. Maxwell, I really didn't think it safe in its present condition. Only—the truth is, I wear it so seldom I kept forgetting."

"Would your daughter have been wearing it, Mrs. Christmas?" she was asked.

Dora shook a doubtful head. "She didn't approve of luxuries and she'd certainly have considered this one. And then it would have looked a bit silly with the sort of clothes she wore, though I suppose no one would have seen in inside the duffel coat. I don't think she'd know about the clasp, and she might have been afraid that if she lost it" (she still spoke of the girl in the present tense, as if she couldn't accustom herself to the truth) "she'd feel responsible. I think, yes, perhaps she would wear it—I simply don't know."

"If the clasp was uncertain it could have become disengaged and dropped off quite apart from any struggle," the police agreed. On the other hand, the circumstances of her death made it seem more probable that she had been wearing it when she was attacked. But if Frankie had really found it where he said he had, then either her murderer had carried her quite a distance to stuff her under the bush—which didn't make sense—or she had shed it accidentally before she was attacked.

Meantime, they'd got Frankie under lock and key, though no actual charge concerning the girl had yet been brought. But everyone, Frankie included, knew what loomed ahead of him as clearly as the path of the righteous leading to the eternal day. And after that the Deluge!

Vi

CROOK HEARD THE NEWS of Frankie's rearrest in the bar of the Golden Goose that evening.

"Oh well," he said, "it was always a case of when rather than if. Wonder how long it'll be before they start suggesting he knows more about our murders than he'll say."

"They haven't said aught yet," Fred pointed out.

"Give 'em time," advised Crook. "They don't like to be hustled."

"What makes you think they may try to tie him up with them, Mr. Crook?"

"Did you ever know a rozzer refuse to shoot a sitting duck?" Crook seemed genuinely surprised.

"If you're walking along a narrow path and there's a duck in your road, you have to do something to shift it," offered Doyle in his mild way.

"If that's the shape of things to come, Frankie might be glad to be getting police protection," Crook opined, "and whatever else he's not getting he'll get that. Probably put a copper in his cell to hold his hand while he's asleep," he added recklessly. "If anyone hereabouts gets it into his noodle that Frankie's really responsible for the old lady's death . . ." It was significant that he didn't mention Freda Woods, though you might have thought her murder would have excited the greater compassion; but it wasn't so, not in these parts anyway. The inquest had been opened and adjourned while the police continued their inquiries, and Dora had taken the dead girl back to lie beside her father in the little churchyard on the windy hillside. It had seemed to her a not much colder place than the world had proved to be to her unfortunate daughter.

"She'd like to think she was beside him," she told Bill simply. "They were very close in life."

Crook was staying put till after Mrs. Nicky's funeral, though he didn't attend in person. He'd never known the dead woman and he didn't approve of muscling in, and though he didn't see how he could be of any further assistance to the local police force (not that they considered he'd been of much assistance anyway), it seemed to him a mark of respect to wait till the old lady was underground. There was a big turn-out for her—shops closed till midday and the whole of the local witches' coven attending in full strength. Ancient black hats, rusty stoles and shoes the like of which hadn't been seen in a shop window for thirty years were all on view. Royalty, thought Crook, watching the procession from his window, could hardly have done better.

He sighed as he prepared to make his way back to London, and that was uncharacteristic, because as a rule he was raring to go. But he had that sense of unease known to neurotic housewives who start having doubts just after they board the Channel boat about the gas and the electricity—did they remember to turn it off? leave the iron on? He'd have told you he wasn't superstitious, but these extra days up north did seem rather a waste of time if they were to end in a tame return to the metropolis.

"I've missed out on something somewhere," he decided, hauling down his battered suitcase and beginning to pack after the competent but unsatisfactory manner of bachelors—that is to say, everything went in, but by the time they came out they'd look as if a mule had been sleeping on them.

Someone tapped on the door and Mrs. Fred entered. She was carrying a cup of tea, and Crook groaned. The British must be the most courageous people on earth, he reflected, seeing how much of the stuff they contrived to put away. His glance wandered to a potted plant in the corner, that somehow didn't look as healthy now as it had done a few days before, and no wonder, considering how much char it had absorbed. If even plants couldn't take it, Crook thought, how could you expect it of the human race?

"Drink it while it's hot," Mrs. Fred encouraged him. "I must admit I'll sleep more easy in my bed of nights now I know they've got the young chap who did for that poor girl."

"Is that what they're saying?" Crook murmured, taking the teacup and putting it on one side.

"Stands to reason," Mrs. Fred argued.

"If they're right and I had any say in the matter, defense or anything, I'd plump for insanity," Crook assured her. "Chap must be missing half his marbles if everything we read in the paper's true."

"That was a nice picture they had of you," offered Mrs. Fred, and for once his eyes, round and bright as brandy balls, nearly bulged out of his head.

"Get along!" he exclaimed. "They're not trying to tie me up with this, surely."

She pulled a newspaper out of an enormous apron pocket. And there it was, as large as life and twice as alarming. Well-known London lawyer they called him.

"They should have warned me," said Crook pleasantly. "I'd have had a nice one taken."

"We shall miss you, Mr. Crook," said Mrs. Fred decorously.

"I'll tell you who won't miss me, and that's the rozzers. On my sam, you'd think I was in cahoots with the murderer, not because of what I could tell them but on account of what I couldn't." He stuffed his pajamas into his case with a reckless energy that made her wince. Lucky, really, he hadn't got a wife, he'd have driven the poor lady up the wall. "If I said I saw a face at the window or heard a voice, they'd have given me a medal. Know what surprises me about the police? The way they can sort the wheat from the chaff—this is true, this ain't. It's true that Frankie was in the Poets House that night, ransacked the wardrobe, helped himself to the commissariat, because he says so. It ain't true that he didn't see the girl, because that don't fit in with their theories. It's not logical, sugar. If one half of the story's true, why shouldn't they accept the other? Well, you don't need to answer that one. Because it 'ud mean they'd have to get out on their hunkers and do a bit more work, and if they started on that tack they'd never pull anyone in, would they?"

"Fred was saying last night it wouldn't surprise him if you had a different idea," said the sedate Mrs. Fred.

"I don't have ideas till I'm paid for them," Crook pointed out.

"All the same, we're missing out on something."

He wondered what it was. Mind you, he'd no proof, but he had a hunch they were on the wrong track, and his hunches hardly ever let him down. Sometimes the missing clue was so glaring it was like being dazzled by the sun, you simply couldn't see it. Other times it was a case of too much wood for the trees. Downstairs a bell rang shrilly. Mrs. Fred started.

"I'll have to see who that is," she told Crook. "Don't let your tea get cold."

He waited till he heard her feet going downstairs before tipping the contents of the cup over the long-suffering plant.

"Final baptism of fire," he promised it. "And sooner you than me."

He was just closing his case when Mrs. Fred returned. "It's someone asking for you, Mr. Crook," she said, and from the tone of her voice he knew the visitor was unknown to her.

"If it's a bluebottle I ain't here," he assured her promptly.

"It's a young woman."

"Well!" Crook's eyes widened. "What d'you know?"

"I told her you were leaving for London this morning, but she said she might as well save the fare. Funny," added Mrs. Fred reflectively, "she doesn't look the pushing sort."

"Monniker?" murmured Mr. Crook. "Or is that a secret?"

"Mon . . . ? Oh, name. She didn't say. Wears a wedding ring, though."

"Bully for her," said Crook. "That's something I'm always short of. Well, let's have her up."

"I've put her in the hall," said Mrs. Fred in definitive tones, and he realized that even at his age and with his figure he was regarded as potential dynamite. No female visitors in bedrooms—there was probably a notice somewhere, only he'd overlooked it. He pulled out his immense turnip watch.

"Nice timing," he beamed. "They'll be open" (he meant the Golden Goose, of course) "and a nice drop of something never harmed anyone."

And like that British admiral whose name he could never remember, he metaphorically tossed his bonnet to wind and sea and ran down to meet his fate.

The girl sitting erect on the hall settle would have held the attention of someone far less impressionable than Crook—or would be when she'd parted with the haggard look she wore. Wide gray eyes with dark lashes, fair hair neatly cut and tied back with a ribbon, a heart-shaped face, a beautiful mouth that owed nothing to make-up—surprising, really, a bell hadn't rung when she walked through the door. It was no wonder some of those old boys had lost their heads when they saw Venus rising from the foam.

He stuck out an enthusiastic leg-of-mutton paw. "Name of Crook," he offered. "Wanted to see me?"

"I seem to have been lucky to catch you before you left," said the girl. "I should have followed you to London, of course . . . I'm Ann Piper, I've come to ask you to help Frankie."

"I knew it," exulted Crook. "The missing chord, if you get my meaning. I mean, there has to be a reason for things, doesn't there? And whatever the rozzers may tell you, I'm a reasonable man. Now, we can't talk here, you know the one about walls having ears, we shall have the snug to ourselves this hour of the day . . ." (The snug wasn't what the landlord would have called it, its official name was the saloon bar, which was never occupied except for a few stuffy old gents who'd have withered away in their posh London clubs if their bank balances hadn't withered first. It wasn't the sort of place Crook would have been found in in the ordinary way if you paid him—well, not unless you paid him a whale of a lot, but admirably suited to today's purpose.) So, "Let's you and me go along and do a bit of rearranging of the evidence," he proposed enthusiastically. "Wouldn't surprise me if we were to come up with something . . ." That was his strength, really, he was never put out of countenance by the most unexpected development. He wouldn't even be disconcerted when he found himself bowing to the Recording Angel or Rhadamanthus on the gate or whoever was on duty on the Day of Judgment, and being offered a pass to the heavenly places. According to his way of reckoning, you can't teach an old dog new tricks and those were where he'd been living most of his life.

"I didn't understand at first," the girl said earnestly as they crossed to the Golden Goose, "you were *that* Mr. Crook."

"Why," said Crook, looking genuinely surprised, "are there any others? How come you heard of me, sugar, anyway?"

"It was someone Frankie knew, oh, it's a long time ago now—he got into a jam and would have been hanged, they hanged them in those days, for the murder of an old woman. Only his girl came to you—probably you don't remember . . ."

"Of course I remember," reproved Crook. "It's my job. Name of Lennie?"

"That's right."

"Nearly got himself hanged in spite of me," Mr. Crook brooded, pushing open the door of the Golden Goose. "Never knew a chap so keen to weave his own rope necktie. In here, sugar, and I'll get Jim to set 'em up. Hope your Frankie's got more sense than that one had," he added meaningfully. Though on the evidence to date that appeared to him the acme of wishful thinking.

"You can't expect him to be like a lamb," the girl fired up. "How would you like to be accused of murder?"

"Come to that, has it?" Crook murmured, adjusting a fussy little cushion—some old boy with a bony backside had probably been grateful for that, he reflected.

"If it hasn't it's only a matter of time. And if Frankie says he found those pearls by a puddle in the woods, that's where he found them. The police are like the shops these days, the customer is never right."

He left her to simmer down while he went to see about drinks. He didn't ask her what she wanted, because she was going to have what he thought best for her and like it. When he returned he was followed by Jim with a pint tankard and a double brandy.

"You can do with this, sugar," he encouraged her. "Settles the blood. And then we'll get down to our sums."

"It's my fault, really." She took a gulp of the brandy. "Good heavens, didn't you put anything into this?"

"All this dilution," grumbled Mr. Crook. "It's a crime. No wonder we lost our Empire. Alloy in the silver, water in the beer."

Jim took the tray and oiled out. They were going to miss this character when he went, and no mistake.

"It's all right," Ann assured him. "I prefer it this way."

"How come it was your fault?" Crook wondered.

"Writing to Frankie as I did about Vicky. She'd picked up the idea that he'd deserted us, some spiteful kid—and four's such a difficult age, you know so much but understand so little, and I was writing to Frankie and I just let myself go."

"Now, sugar," said Crook in the tones of a persuasive alligator, "it'll save a lot of time if we both face the fact that your Frankie's a bit of a moron. Only a moron would have slugged that old gent for trying to protect his own property, and only a moron would have made the prison break."

"A moron would have got caught at once," Ann vigorously defended her husband. "And he was thinking of Vicky, not himself. He grew up in an orphanage, he knows what it feels like to be deserted."

Crook nodded thoughtfully. "I didn't know. All the same—I'm not one to bat for the police, as anyone will tell you, but if someone hands you a nice hot dinner on a plate you'd be a gaby to refuse it. And this plate's got everything. Escaped convict, signs of his presence in the old lady's house, which he don't deny, her cash in his hip pocket, young lady's jewels in his bag . . ."

"I'd have thought that alone would have cleared him," cried Ann in scornful tones. "Would a murderer go around carrying deadly evidence like that? Anyway, if he'd so much as laid a finger on her, do you suppose he'd have given me *her* necklace?"

"You don't read enough history," Crook rebuked her. "It's what killers have done all down the ages. Take that chap in the Moat Farm murder—he could have gone to a quiet grave if he hadn't started decking out his fancy pieces with the late Miss Holland's jewelry. Someone was bound to notice."

"But this is all circumstantial," the girl insisted. "It could just as easily have happened the way Frankie says it did, so why don't they start at that end, instead of making up their minds in advance? Of course, it makes it easier for them to say it has to be him, because they haven't winkled out anyone else . . ."

"And you think I'll be able to provide them with a substitute?"

"He exists, we both know that. If it wasn't Frankie, and it wasn't, then it has to be someone. Neither of those women was responsible for what happened to them." She hesitated, took another gulp of the brandy. "I meant to say—they have offered Frankie a certificate of legal aid . . ."

"Unless you want to be responsible for the death of the old boy on the box from heart failure you won't mention legal aid where my name's concerned," Crook warned her. "Your Frankie ain't the only one with a reputation to maintain. Anyway," he added hurriedly, "let's cross that bridge when we come to it. And no sense trying to poke the rozzers in the eye, because public opinion at present is on their side. And don't start blaming them—your Frankie's got a record, remember."

"If you mean the man at Mapledurham, he asked for it. Why shouldn't it be as much of a crime to refuse to help someone in trouble as help yourself to twenty pounds? After all, what was that to him?"

"Twenty pounds," said Crook simply. "And if you're going to make that a crime you're not going to have enough prisons in the country to house the population. As for your Frankie telling you he'd never set eyes on the young lady, well, it's what you'd expect, isn't it? I don't say I don't believe him," he added quickly. "I only work for the innocent, but some circumstantial evidence is very strong, as when you find a trout in the milk. Quotation," he added kindly, seeing her mystified expression.

"He didn't see her," the girl insisted. "Oh, they tried to trip him up—what was she wearing, what did he do with her bag? They haven't even found that yet . . ."

"No reason why they ever should," Crook agreed. "We don't even know that it was chucked away in the vicinity. Come to that, there's no proof she was ever killed in the wood. Could have accepted a lift, not realizing nothing is for free . . ."

"There you are," declared the girl triumphantly. "Frankie couldn't have offered her a lift, he hadn't got a car."

"I thought we'd agreed Frankie wasn't guilty. But the odds are that the chap who put paid to the poor booby's account did travel by car. I've seen the place, it ain't a pedestrian's paradise even by daylight, and by all accounts a nasty lot of chaps get holed up there on occasion. Of course," he added reflectively, "that could be the answer—she stumbled on something she shouldn't and it was too dangerous to let her go on breathing. More people lose their lives for that reason than ever the police will know. Mind you, no one's come forward with a story of seeing a car . . ."

"Well, would you? Simply an invitation to the police to switch suspicions. And who wants to be mixed up with a murder?"

"Nice to see you've got your head screwed on right," Crook congratulated her. But he knew it didn't amount to much, really. Dames got an idea, and it was easier to shift the Rock of Gibraltar than get them to admit they could be mistaken—that was his experience—while logic was a word they couldn't spell. Not that he regretted it. A world run by logic would be pretty unexciting.

"He couldn't tell them anything," the girl continued, "and you can be sure they pulled every conceivable rabbit out of the hat."

"And he didn't recognize one of them? I don't blame him. Rabbits are like the Chinese, they all look alike to us—though, of course, that don't go for other rabbits."

"And even if he had met her, which he didn't, he was miles away on the Monday night, he didn't have to kill her."

"Say she recognized him?"

"Why should she? In the middle of a dark wood? And anyhow, all he had to do was walk away. What could she do then?"

"Inform on him."

Ann laughed abruptly. "He'd have been in the next county before she could contact the police."

"I wouldn't be too sure," Crook warned her. "There's a phone booth about a mile down the road. All she had to do was dial 999 and he could have found both ends of the earth stopped when he got there. And though I haven't met him yet, I've seen his picture, and I'd say it wasn't a face it 'ud be easy to forget."

Her own softened suddenly, her armor fell away, she showed herself young, vulnerable, racked with fear. "I see it all the time," she confessed.

"And then there was the old lady coming back through the wood, like the Jabberwock, hirpling as she came. You'd hear a mastodon of a car like that the way you'd hear an elephant trampling through the undergrowth. She most likely opened her mouth to scream, and X tried to shut it for her, and didn't recognize his own strength. If he'd stopped there, the odds are he wouldn't be facing anything worse than a charge of manslaughter, though that's bad enough. Murder has to be aforethought. Too bad about the pearls. Lady says the catch was loose—I suppose they came off in the struggle and no one noticed."

"Well, of course no one noticed. If he had he'd have tipped them into the ditch, and Frankie wouldn't have touched them."

"It isn't what chaps do that brings them a life sentence, it's what they forget."

"No one's really discovered what she was doing there in the first place."

"Now, sugar, be your age, we know what she was doing there, she was running away from home. Why she should be in that neck of the woods—well, like I said, she probably got a lift, wouldn't play ball, threatened to make trouble. I'd say she was a born troublemaker, and when they do it in the name of righteousness, well, that's the worst kind. In short, she'd got herself tied up like a kitten in a tree—couldn't go up, couldn't get down. She was like Felix, she had to keep on walking, and it was her bad luck she had to walk right into a deathtrap. So—the police are asking for a motive. Your Frankie has one ready-made."

"So has someone else," insisted the girl.

"You never let go, do you?" said Crook.

"If you were hanging on to a cliff by your fingertips you wouldn't let go either."

Crook thought privately he wouldn't ever find himself in such a position, but no sense trying to labor that point now. "Does he know about your coming here—Frankie, I mean?"

"I told him I'd get him a lawyer, the best there is. I told him, too, not to talk to anyone first, but I suppose they egged him on."

"Why, d'you mean he'd have told a different story if he'd seen me?" Crook sounded surprised.

"It might have sounded different," said the girl shrewdly.

"Ah well." Crook made as if to start clearing the decks. "A lot's going to depend on your Frankie now. You can take a horse to water, but you can't make him drink."

"You can pour the stuff down his throat, can't you?" the girl demanded.

"Only if you're prepared to take the chance of having a hand bitten off in the process. Still, what's it to you if I go around minus a hand for the rest of my days so long as Frankie keeps both his?"

"I always heard you were the kind that doesn't take no for an answer."

"Know all the answers yourself, don't you?" murmured Mr. Crook. "If that's the type you're after you only have to take a looksee in the glass any time."

"If you just walk in and tell him everything's fixed, so it's no use his wasting his breath . . ."

"It might be a case of the third corpse lying out on the shining sand," Crook agreed.

"And even if he'd tried to silence the girl and—and overdone it, he'd never have attacked the old woman, and you can see the way the official mind is working. Don't ask me how I know, Mr. Crook, I do know, I'm his wife."

"Mightn't have had much choice," Crook told her soberly. "It's a rum thing how often B does follow A. Here's this girl—well, that's bad enough, but no witness, cut and run—and then along comes the old lady, and she's the kind with a social conscience too. If you're shoving a body under a bush, it's a bit difficult to pretend it's the remains of your picnic basket. And you get funny weather up here, dark one minute, silver-bright the next. Oh no, if the old lady had any suspicions, she's the kind that would have contacted the police. It might sound like Nosey Parkering to you, but she'd see it different."

"So she gave the murderer a lift back to the Poets House? Mr. Crook, it doesn't make sense."

"Well, we don't know what he told her, do we? Say he said he'd found the girl's body, wanted to contact the police, could even have offered himself as an escort . . ."

"A man the police were after?"

"We're not assuming it was Frankie. It's the way I'd play it myself. And murderers are just ordinary men and women who've got into a jam, it's not a profession. Cain could have worn a seal on his forehead, but the Lord God don't make things that simple for people nowadays. Some of the nice quiet folk who've picked up a hammer or collected a dose of prussic acid and put it to what they thought was the best account—it 'ud surprise you. You should go and see the waxworks in the Chamber of Horrors sometime, all murderers the ones I have in mind, and there ain't many you wouldn't ask in for a cup of tea on a hot day. No, it could be the chap's hand was forced. If he was going to save his own neck he had to break hers. That kind of thing happens more often than you'd guess."

"But all this happened on Monday," the girl pressed. "Frankie wasn't in the neighborhood until Tuesday."

"That's his story."

"But if he'd been responsible for two corpses, he'd have put a county between him and them."

"Might be smart to stay put. That's the way they'll argue, anyhow. The house was closed, remember, there ain't much traffic on that road, he was probably dead beat, could be he was waiting for the dark. Just bad luck for him I came by and saw the lamp." He stood up. "Now, sugar, take that worried look off your face. No sense two of us having kittens. And you've got the little girl to consider."

She nodded. "That's all I can do for Frankie now—look after Vick. It doesn't seem enough."

Mr. Crook looked a little startled. He wasn't accustomed to being quite so convincingly wiped off the slate. "Well, don't underestimate yourself," he said. "You've pulled me in, haven't you? Got yourself a partner, though I'll be lucky if your chap don't throw me out on my ear. Still, I have ears an elephant might envy." He rubbed one of them in a reflective fashion. "Where do I find you in an emergency?" She gave him an address, which he wrote down.

"How about you?" she asked.

"You've dumped this in my lap," said Mr. Crook, "and that's where we'll leave it. If you should get any bright ideas you can ring this number." He gave her one of his outrageous cards. "If I'm not available Bill will take a message. But you don't hire a dog and bark yourself, and any barking that needs to be done I'll do. And I have a pretty resonant bark, they tell me," he added encouragingly.

She nodded. "I'll wear my muzzle till you say I can take it off," she promised. "Sometimes," she added unexpectedly, "I envy nuns in convents, they save themselves so much trouble."

"Well, that's what we're told man's born to," Crook reminded her cozily. "Pity to miss the purpose of your being."

They weren't in the least alike, but she reminded him of his mum. After Crook Senior had just walked out of the house one day and somehow lost the way back, Mrs. C. had taken everything in hand, including their son, and if the Amazons were anything like her, it wasn't surprising they'd scared the pants off their male foes. She was really the main reason why Crook could still put bachelor on his income tax returns. He could face an army of police and/or criminals, but not the prospect of a second woman in his life who might prove a carbon copy of the first. Mincemeat may be very tasty to the one who's eating the tart, but it can't be much fun for the minced. And when it came to millstones, a devoted wife could be worse than a dead albatross. His heart burned for Frankie, though within forty-eight hours it might be burning even more fiercely for himself.

vii

SINCE HIS RECAPTURE and return to Cumberton Prison, Frankie had been accorded the distinction of a cell to himself. He was now regarded as potentially dangerous, since in addition to the crime for which he had been originally sentenced, it was now clear he was shortly to face trial for murder. When the warder came to tell him he had a visitor he found Frankie lying on the bed with his back to the door and his hands behind his head.

"Tell him to buggar off!" said Frankie inelegantly. "When I want visitors I'll send for them. Or hasn't your governor ever heard of privacy?"

"Gentleman's come a long way," offered the warder, not coaxing but sounding grimly amused.

Frankie discerned the amusement and didn't care for it. "Gentleman waits for an invitation," he snapped.

"I'll tell him you're not interested then, shall I?"

"If it's that Purves trying to muscle in again . . ." Purves was the prison visitor Frankie had steadfastly refused to see.

"The card says Crook," the warder told him. Treating a prisoner like Frankie Piper with kid gloves on went against the grain, but he didn't fancy going back to Crook with Frankie's message.

Frankie swung his legs down and came to his feet, a compact little dark bull of a man, so that in a way it seemed surprising he didn't carry horns. When he saw the oversized card in the warder's hand he said, "Is that it?"

"Bit oversized, isn't it?" the warder agreed. "But everything about that man is outsized."

85

"What's he want?" Frankie still sounded suspicious.

"If you was to see him you could ask him, couldn't you?"

The warder was another dark little fellow, with an astute cockney face; whatever had driven him into the prison service it hadn't been a sense of vocation. He was as sharp as a dickybird, the kind that will put out its mother's eyes to get a succulent worm.

"I know about him," Frankie said.

"Well, don't ask me for sympathy. We're all in the same boat."

"What I don't understand is what he's doing here."

"According to him he's come to see you."

Frankie looked up accusingly. "Nobody asked him. Unless— this isn't any of your doing? The governor, I mean?"

"Do me a favor," pleaded the warder. "We've got enough on our plates in this institution without inviting a troublemaker like that to drop in."

"Well, what do you know?" Suddenly Frankie grinned, though there wasn't much amusement behind it. "May as well, I suppose. Might be good for a laugh."

When he found himself face to face with Crook he went into his clown's routine. "Mr. Crook? I don't believe we've met."

"Could have done," said Crook. "Funny to think if that curtain had been properly pulled I'd never have known you were at the Poets House that night, and you might still be wandering fancy-free." (Though he clearly didn't think that likely.) "Like some poet says, the little more and how much it is."

"D'you charge extra for the wisecracks?" Frankie wanted to know. "And since we're on the subject . . ."

"Why am I here? On your wife's instructions."

Frankie's face changed like lightning, it was like watching a dark cloud roll over the sky. "I told her . . ."

"When you're half my age and have a tenth of my experience you won't waste your breath telling women what to do and what not to do, because they'll do it anyway. She's got the idea you don't know anything about either of those two dames, except what you read in the paper or heard over the radio."

"She's dead right."

Crook nodded. "That's what I thought, too. Well, I'm a chap with his living to get, I can't afford to work for the guilty, can I? Even when I only work for the innocent the police don't love me like a brother."

"They will do it, won't they?" observed Frankie, following his own line of thought and shoving his hands into his pockets. "Try to arrange your life for you, I mean? I told Ann . . ."

"She couldn't make a more thundering mess of it than you've made on your own," Crook pointed out brutally. "Look, admitted you're the kingpin of your own situation, right, but to me you're just another name on the board, so let's cut the cackle and get down to brass tacks. And if you were thinking of getting on your high horse and saying you can manage very nicely without me, thank you, I shall know you're a liar and I shan't believe anything else you tell me."

Frankie sat down in rather a dazed fashion. "You do go on, don't you?" he said. "Like that night you came thundering at the door. God, I thought you were never going away. If you'd left me in peace instead of spreading the news—come to think of it, maybe Ann's right, you do owe us a life."

Crook regarded him with open admiration. "That's a new line," he said. "I'm always out for a novelty. Now, can we start? And from the beginning, if you don't mind. I'm no thought reader, though I can add two and two and make it four, and there are fewer of us able to do that than you might suppose. Ninety-four's nearer most of their totals."

"Classing me with the morons?" Frankie suggested.

"You can't be altogether a moron or you'd never have got away from Cumberton in the first place, or at least not for more than an hour or two. It has the name of being a jail where no one stays at liberty more than twenty-four hours except the ones who've stepped right out of line into the swamp and joined the coffin queue."

"That lot haven't got the sense they were born with," Frankie agreed. "They will take the path behind the prison because it's comparatively protected, whereas the front's as open as a cricket pitch. So what happens? They run straight into the bogs, and back they come, dead or alive. One of these days they'll think of importing a few crocs and then the warders won't even have to get their feet wet hauling the corpses home."

"And you went over the wall and across the road?" Crook nodded. "It would take a bit of nerve, what with the traffic and the openness and the searchlights that would sweep the whole area. You wouldn't think a chap had a chance."

"Secret is time," Frankie explained. "First thing, they don't expect you to take that way, so they concentrate on the back. Of course, once they realize what your game is they lay it all on—searchlights, bloody great bell, dogs, the lot. So that everyone within a mile knows some chap is out for his life and grabs the first weapon that comes to hand—hatchet, stick, anything 'ull do—and comes out to join the hunt. Well, why not, why should the nobs have all the fun?"

"You must have moved like greased lightning," suggested Crook diplomatically.

"Anyone 'ud think you got a medal for turning a chap in. I had one bit of luck, I'd managed to lift a raincoat some screw had left lying around, so the first fellow I met outside thought I was on the hunt, too. 'One of those bastards got away,' he yelled to me. 'It's not safe for decent people, having that prison so near.' If I'd had the time to spare," added Frankie deliberately, "I'd have choked him."

The depth of feeling in his voice shocked the older man. "That's one of the things not to say when you're on the stand," he warned him.

"They were so sure I'd follow the usual procedure they didn't turn the dogs loose right away. That gave me my chance to get across the road into the woods and over the water. Don't they say water wrecks the scent?"

"It wrecks practically everything, come to that," agreed Crook briskly. "Bridge handy? That was convenient."

"Bridge nothing," retorted Frankie scornfully. "But you soon lose your modesty in stir. Still, you wouldn't know about that, would you?"

"I'm here to find out what you know," Crook pointed out. "Not to be told about my ignorance. What next?"

"After I crossed the river I walked for a while, then I got on a local train packed with chaps coming back from a factory. It was too soon for the alarm to be general and we were jammed like sardines anyway. That way you never see your neighbor's face. I could have been invisible."

"How did you manage about a ticket?" asked Crook practically.

"There was a folding purse in the raincoat pocket. Not much in it, but enough to get me started."

"Don't mind taking chances, do you, chum?" Crook murmured. "Filching a prison officer's property, breaking into a bank—because that's what it will sound like when it comes into court—What happened to the raincoat?"

"Ditched it in a phone booth," said Frankie. "Nothing special about it, and I'd got a change of clobber by then. Hit a market the next morning—well, I slept rough the night before but you can't win them all, can you?—sort of place where you buy ready-mades off a rail. There was a chap there trying on some of the jackets. 'Here, you can't do that,' the fellow told him. 'You tell me your size, we've got the lot.' 'Expect me to buy a pig in a poke, do you?' said the other. 'If it's pigs you're wanting you've come to the wrong shop,' the fellow said. Quite an artist, that chap. Oh, it was a regular argy-bargy. I've wondered a lot what he thought when he turned round and found his jacket was missing. Had to buy a new one, I suppose. Outside a radio shop I heard them bellowing the news—authorities were warning all housewives in the Cumberton area not to open their doors to strangers, I was a dangerous chap, chop your kid up into six bits and eat him for breakfast. Tell you one thing, Mr. Crook. I wouldn't mind being one of the keepers of the lake of fire and brimstone, or doing the stoking. Woman next to me was t'ach-ing and t'cha-ing, these awful men, life wasn't safe for decent people, didn't I think? 'You're right,' I told her, 'I'd shoot 'em like mad dogs if I had my way. Don't know why you and me should have to pay taxes to keep 'em alive. Fancy wanting to see your own kid when it was ill, it's downright unnatural.' "

"Your defense is going to cost me more than a headache," Crook warned him. "Well, get on with it."

He took his difficult client step by step through his story. As he'd anticipated, there was precious little to help and a lot to hinder. Frankie couldn't identify most of the places where he claimed to have spent the nights. On the fatal Monday night he claimed to have been in a barn, hoping to goodness the farmer wouldn't flush him out. "All those ruddy sheep," he said, "if they'd started coughing . . . It might be a good idea for Ann to put a fair space between her and the past, but why did she have to go to world's end? You know, they were at her to change her name, but she told them, 'You've taken away enough of mine, haven't you? You can leave me that.'"

Crook diplomatically let that ride. "Now tell about the pearls," he invited.

"I found them, like I said. I was walking along behind the hedge, I'd had a lift from a funny sort of chap, curious, you know, and there's times you prefer your own company. Not that there was so much traffic on the road, but there's always the odd car or lorry, and I knew the road ran through to a main artery and I thought I might get a milk train or something. I was pretty short of cash and I could have done with a meal, they button their pockets pretty close in the north. Then I noticed that coming through the hedge I'd caught my hand on a thorn bush and it was bleeding a bit, so when I saw this pond affair I stopped to bathe it. And it was then that I saw the pearls, if that's what they really are. They were lying quite deep in the grass, you could walk past and never see them. Even so, if the moon hadn't suddenly shone out they could be there still. I didn't think much about them at first, then it seemed a pity to waste them, they looked ordinary enough but not common, if you get me, and you can't buy your wife much in the way of presents on what they pay you in stir. So I shoved them into my pocket, and afterward I dropped them into the bag. To tell you the truth, I'd forgotten I had them, when that chap pulled them out of the case— The girl must have been nutty," he added simply.

"She's dead now," Crook reminded him, "and we don't know that the pearls had anything to do with that."

Frankie looked sullen. "Well, there it is," he said. "You know the rest. How do you like it?"

"I've heard yarns I like better," Crook told him frankly. "It would help if you could produce a single witness to a single statement, but perhaps that's too much to anticipate."

"Much too much," Frankie agreed. "Well, hell, you don't suppose any law-abiding citizen wants to see his picture in the paper as accessory after the fact—that's what he'd be called. And even if one of them wouldn't mind coming forward in the interests of justice"—his mobile mouth twisted cynically—"I bet he'd be a married man . . ."

"And his wife won't want her picture in the paper. You could be right. What made you pick on the Poets House?"

"Like I told the police, it was empty, it was dark, there was no one around, and I was sick of pigsties. I saw this road leading away from the lane, and it didn't seem likely I'd meet any traffic there. I thought, This is God's gift to the refugee."

"Made yourself at home there, didn't you?" suggested Crook.

Frankie stared. "It was closed for the winter. I wasn't in anyone's way."

"Didn't wonder about finding forty quid in an empty house? People going off for the winter usually take their bank balances with them."

"It could have been left for decorators or something. I mean, there was this key to the back door. Anyway, I didn't stop to worry about that. It was the first break I'd had since I got away from Cumberton. And people that can afford to leave forty quid lying around in an open drawer aren't exactly paupers. Well, Mr. Crook, how are we coming?"

"If you'd given your mind to it you couldn't have found me a more unpromising story," Crook assured him genially. He raised a few points, checked up some details, then rose to go. "And just remember I ain't the young lady called Bright whose movements were quicker than light. The Lord God may have created the world in seven days, but I don't work on His wave length. Try and keep your nose clean, you've got a list of charges against you as long as my arm, and wait for the message. This chap . . ."

"Which chap?"

Crook stared. "Haven't you been listening? The chap who's responsible for two murders, because, though it's a record when I agree with the police, I believe they're right this time in tacking the two together. It ain't you, it wasn't an Act of God, so it must be Mr. X, and unless he's dropped himself down a well or strung himself up behind a door, he's still available."

"And you're going to find him, just like that?" Frankie snapped his fingers.

"If you ever say your prayers," retorted Crook, "you pray I find him before he finds me. One thing, he believes he's got away with murder, and that's when they start getting careless."

"Your carelessness, our opportunity," paraphrased Frankie.

"I couldn't have put it more neat myself," Crook agreed.

And off he went, merry as a grig, out once more on the old trail, the long trail, the trail that is always new.

Dr. Gordon Glass crackled the sheets of the *Record*, and reading from the headlines, demanded cheerfully, "Is medicine the Aunt Sally of the professions? You tell me. Not that I don't feel sometimes that I operate a freak show. What is it, D?"

For his wife had paused in her task of refilling his cup and was staring past him with an incredulous air. "I don't believe it," she said. "Unless he's come to the wrong address. Who does he think we are? Madame Tussaud?"

Her husband turned his head in time to see an immense yellow car such as is seldom beheld on sea or land draw up at the gate. Out of it stepped an immense figure rolled in an ulster of fearsome design, and this creature apparently was making for their gate.

"Toad of Toad Hall," said the doctor quickly. "Never mind about the tea. You put him on his way. I shall have freaks enough at morning surgery."

"On the other hand," suggested Doreen, "he could be a millionaire. Surely only a millionaire would dare go round in that setup."

Mr. Toad swung open the gate and came striding up the path.

"What that chap wants is a trick cyclist," said the doctor firmly. "Anyway, what's he doing being conscious this hour of the morning? I thought only doctors and their patients came awake before nine-thirty."

"You can't leave me to cope," Doreen protested.

"I have a date to hear the fifth installment of Miss Bennett's love life," her husband explained. "I tell you, D, your education's been neglected—if she can manage all this without even one husband . . ." He dodged behind her chair, out of the French windows, and so around to the garage.

The front doorbell rang as though to summon guilty souls to judgment. The shiver that ran through Doreen seemed to echo through the house. She flung into the hall, pulled the door open a few inches and said, "Did you want the doctor? I'm afraid he's at the surgery. In any case, this is his private entrance."

The apparition opened a mouth almost large enough for a hippopotamus. "Do I look as though I needed a doctor—professionally, I mean?" boomed Mr. Crook, yanking out one of his cards.

"And he doesn't allow me to buy on H.P.," Doreen continued, pretending not to notice it.

"I'm not here to sell," Mr. Crook explained.

"More like an inquiry perhaps?" Doreen offered.

Mr. Crook beamed. "Just the ticket."

"We don't answer questions either." Doreen started to close the door.

"I bet you answered the police," said Mr. Crook, and she stiffened.

"Are you the press?"

"Do I look like the press?"

Privately she thought he looked like something out of the zoo.

"We'd get there a lot quicker if you'd cast your peepers over this," he urged, pushing the card at her so that she couldn't refuse to take it. "He'd have pushed it down the front of my blouse," she told her husband afterward. Talk about the Kingdom of Heaven suffering violence and the violent taking it by force. Arthur G. Crook, she read, and a medley of addresses and telephone numbers. Your Trouble, Our Opportunity. We Never Close.

"Is it a joke?" she asked weakly.

"Well, not to Frankie Piper it isn't."

At the sound of that name it was as if the hall were suddenly filled with hailstones of pure ice.

"You're here in connection with that man?" The last words seemed to have a capital-letter connotation. That Man people said in the war, meaning Adolf Hitler. He'd hardly heard so much hate in a human voice since those distant days.

"Representing him," Crook acknowledged. "Well, he needs someone to hold his hand."

"I've nothing to say." Once let the creature invade the house and it would be like those science-fiction horrors; already in imagination she saw the walls start to crack, the fungus bloom. "A young thug kills an old woman . . ."

"Who says?" asked Mr. Crook.

"The police."

"And Frankie says he didn't. And Frankie should know."

"You mean, you *believe* him?"

"I think he should have a fair crack of the whip." In her indignation Doreen had moved backward and Crook came smartly past her into the hall. "Never believe in discussing your business on doorsteps," he told her. "Walls aren't in it when it comes to ears. No," he went on, "since you ask me, I don't think Frankie did kill your Aunt Abby. I don't think he's got the intelligence— well, not the right kind anyway. If it had been just the girl I might have second thoughts. Nice hall you have here," he added politely.

"Since you're in," said Doreen, and her guardian angel couldn't have pretended she sounded gracious, "you'd better come this way." She opened the door of what was known as the general-purposes room; everything that couldn't be housed anywhere else had been pushed in here. Crook looked about him appreciatively. Flotsam and jetsam. It suited him a treat.

"I don't know how you suppose I can help," insisted Doreen.

"I do like to get my info at first-hand," Crook explained. He put down the hideous brown bowler he had whipped off when she opened the door, and she saw his hair was as thick and red as a fox's. Probably had all a fox's cunning too, she reflected. "Now, this call you made to your auntie on the Monday night."

"Clanger number one," said Doreen crisply. "I didn't ring her, someone rang me."

That was the way Crook had heard it, too, but it was always nice to have your impressions reinforced, and women loved to put you in the wrong.

"Give a name?" he asked.

"He said he was the doctor."

"Ah, but which doctor?"

"He could have said he was the Apostle Paul and I wouldn't have been any wiser. Aunt Abby didn't believe in doctors. She said she'd lived according to nature for years, and nature had never let her down, and when her time came she'd be ready. She said she'd seen too many synthetic ghosts being kept alive like old toys . . ."

"Sans teeth, sans lungs, sans guts, sans everything," Mr. Crook agreed. He nodded. "She had something there. And yet you weren't suspicious."

"There was no particular reason why I should be. I knew she wasn't as fit as she supposed. I'd seen her less than a month before, and that was when I insisted she should come and spend the winter with us. You've seen the house, of course? Then you know it's not the least suitable for an old woman."

"But that's just what she wasn't," Crook demurred. "And all the locals agree about that. Timeless and free—that was your Aunt Abby," he wound up, taking an unexpected leap into poesy.

"She may have been all that in spirit, but physically she was in very poor shape. I'm a doctor's wife, I should know. Or hadn't you heard?"

"I'd heard," said Mr. Crook.

"I tried to persuade her to see a doctor when I was up there, but I might as well have been Canute ordering the sea to retire. Well, I thought if she was with us, Gordon, my husband, could form some sort of opinion— I was very fond of her," she added defiantly.

"In good company at that," Crook agreed. "What did this character say—this Dr. Whosit?"

"He said my aunt had had a slight attack, and he didn't think it wise for her to travel for a day or two. Not to worry, *anno domini* . . ."

"Attack of what?" inquired Crook shrewdly.

"He didn't go into details. I asked if she should go into hospital, and he said oh no, not necessary, he'd get the nurse to come in—she was in bed and he'd given her a sedative, everything was under control. I said my husband was a doctor and we could come up and collect her as soon as she was fit to come. And I said

I hoped she'd remember to cancel Benson's car. Well, there was no point his coming over and disturbing her if she couldn't make use of him."

"Very helpful," Crook agreed cryptically. "There was a card on the mantelpiece from Benson, so he'd know the phone number. And he relayed your message all right—about your husband coming up, I mean. Only somehow Benson got the idea it was your husband speaking."

"I expect he got it muddled," said Doreen vaguely, but Crook told her, "Do you? I think he got the message right. Well, if they thought your husband was there they wouldn't bother, would they? But if she was on her owney-oh—they think a lot of your auntie up in that part of the world. I tell you, I was there for the funeral. It was like Covent Garden."

Doreen sniffed. "She wouldn't have approved of that."

"What's on your mind?" asked Crook keenly.

"I didn't say . . ."

"You didn't have to."

"You don't miss much, do you? Well then, I was anxious about her. It was as if she knew something, suspected something—she was so unwilling to come, and yet last winter she came and she quite enjoyed herself."

"Had a hunch maybe. I have them myself."

"You should tell my husband that. He thinks they're all poppycock."

"Who's he to denigrate poppycock? Old lady didn't speak to you herself?"

"She was in bed, and the only telephone is in the hall. She wouldn't have an extension in her room, so obviously she wouldn't get up and come down. I did ring the next morning, but there was no answer, and I supposed she was still in bed, and then I waited, expecting to hear from the doctor—I'd no reason to suppose he wasn't the genuine article."

"I read a story once," said Crook, "about a chap who got inside a chimpanzee's skin and went to visit a lady who'd annoyed him. The minute he came into the room she started to yell blue murder. I mean, she never stopped to find out if it was a real chimpanzee."

"Nor would I in those circumstances," said Doreen honestly. "What happened to her?"

"Oh," said Crook, who'd invented the story on the spur of the moment. "She went mad, spent the rest of her life thinking everyone but herself was a chimpanzee. Needn't have been so far wrong either," he added, "not wishing to knock the chimps, of course. He didn't say anything else that might give you a clue?"

"I tell you, he spoke exactly like a real doctor."

"I'm like your Aunt Abby," said Crook. "I don't have much truck with the profession. Do they talk different from the rest of us?"

"They have a sort of professional confidence." Suddenly she grinned. "You should know."

"Any chance you'd recognize the voice again if you were to hear it?"

Doreen simply stared. "A voice I'd heard for less than five minutes over a long-distance phone? Have you the least idea, Mr. Crook, how many telephone calls a doctor's wife takes out of hours, when the receptionist is off duty? No, I wouldn't know it again, and it was probably disguised anyway."

"No, why?" asked Mr. Crook. "If the chap was a stranger to you. Besides, it may be all right for actors to put on an act, it's their job, but these amateurs always overdo it."

"What I still can't fathom," cried Doreen, "is why anyone thought it necessary to put her out of the way. She was nobody's enemy."

"She was an honest woman, wasn't she, and honest people are their own enemies, *per se*. Naturally, no one wants to kill an old lady from choice, but the way I see it his arm was being twisted. Even the police have worked that one out."

"Because of the girl. But we don't know that the two crimes were connected."

"I'm like the White Queen," conceded Crook, "I can believe six impossible things before breakfast—and we all know nature's prodigal, but she's not as prodigal as that. Oh no, they tie up all right, and it was just your auntie's bad luck she should turn up the minute she did."

"Where do we go from here?" demanded Doreen impatiently.

"You can't suppose this man will come forward."

"If he was going to do that, Frankie Piper wouldn't be needing me. No, we have to winkle him out— But even the Israelites couldn't make bricks without straw, and I'm going round like those maddening birds that pick up a bit here and a bit there till they've got enough to line a nest."

"And you think you'll be successful?"

"I wouldn't like to think a bird could do better than me," returned Crook modestly. "Funny thing is I don't believe it was ever necessary to knock her out."

"But if she'd seen the girl . . ."

"Who says she did? The body was found under a bush. I've seen the place, no one driving at night would have recognized it. No, what your Aunt Abby saw was a man standing near a bush where, sooner or later, a girl's body was going to be found. And when she heard that, she was going to remember . . ."

"You're not suggesting she'd recognize a strange man seen for a minute under such conditions?"

"Well, that's the point," said Crook, "was he a strange man? Would she have given a stranger a lift back to her own house, particularly if she thought he was up to a bit of no good?"

"Perhaps he threatened her. She was an old woman, un-armed . . ."

"Oh, use your marbles," said Crook kindly. "She was armed with one of the best weapons man's ever invented, she was driving a car. A ton or so of metal can knock you out as nice and neat as any popgun, and we know he wasn't armed . . ."

"How do we know?"

"If he'd had a weapon he'd have used it," said Crook. "He'd have been crazy not to. And if it was Frankie, we know they don't issue lethal weapons in H.M. prisons and he'd had no chance of picking one up en route. If he had, someone would remember."

"He could have insisted on getting a lift," Doreen opined.

"Well, even so. Say he was a stranger, she had no call to drive him back to her house, about a black mile and a half from any living thing except a few wet cows, and just wait to be banged over the head. Not your auntie. She simply had to turn left and

whiz him along to the nearest police station. If he was a stranger
—Frankie, say—he wouldn't be any the wiser. But if it was a local
and she recognized him, then she'd accept his story, that he
wanted to contact the police and she had a phone . . ."

"You mean, he told her there was a dead girl . . . ?"

"I don't know, do I?" said Crook reasonably. "But at least it
makes sense. Ever walk over a quicksand? Well, I did once—
well, not to say over, but I put one great beetle crusher in, and
blow me down, I thought I was never going to get it out again.
And everything on the surface looking as nice as pie. It's surprising what you can uncover if you rootle a bit. Now and again
when some chap asks me the way or thumbs a lift, I find myself
thinking, You may look like Sir Galahad but for all I know you're
last week's murderer or the one who'll qualify for the office on
Monday. No, if it had been a chap like Frankie and he'd been
afraid she'd shop him, he'd have knocked her off in the wood, left
her at the wheel, made his getaway—how long before she was
found, do you suppose? Not till next day at earliest, and by that
time Frankie would be out of earshot, and why should anyone
pick on him, except on the ground of giving a dog a bad name?"

"So what do we do next?" demanded Doreen.

"I snout around a bit more," Crook told her. "And if luck's on
my side I might turn up the invisible witness."

"The . . . ?"

"The chap—or dame—you haven't allowed for, because you
couldn't know he or she was goin' to surface. You'd be surprised,
sugar, how often the slops get the credit for pulling in a criminal
when the real bonanza should go to the I.W. Remember the
Burning Car case? No, before your time, perhaps, but Rouse laid
his plan very nice, got a body that's never been identified,
slugged it, left it in his car and set the whole thing alight. Hoping
to be taken for the cadaver, see? And then two young perishers
come walking over the hill, returning from a dance, and see the
bonfire, and it's no more a case of Bob's your uncle, but Bob's
your Uncle Death. Oddest case that ever came my way," he
added, improvising madly, "was a chap whose wife annoyed
him to such a pitch he couldn't think of any solution but pushing
her out of a window. Chose his time and place with care—nice

quiet streets, no rozzers, neighbors all abed by eleven P.M.—look, angel, see the lovely moon, and then, tip over arse. Couldn't go wrong."

"But it did?"

Crook nodded. "Another exasperated husband, afraid he might follow suit, got up at two A.M. on the ground that wifie's pet Peke wanted to go tatas, and came round the corner just in time to get a ringside view of what happened."

"And he went to the police?"

Crook looked surprised. "Well, he was a righteous citizen, wasn't he? If he hadn't been he'd have served his wife likewise. Not that it helped him much, because unfortunately when the lady fell she fell, all eleven stone of her, poor Pekie never had a chance, you could have pushed his silhouette through a keyhole. When master got back from the station with his story, the wife was so infuriated—any man worth his salt would have let himself be flattened sooner than leave the burden to a pore innocent animal—that she crowned him with a scent bottle—best cut glass, everything was high tone in that establishment—they do say Pekie had the more impressive funeral of the two."

"I don't believe a word of it," gasped Doreen.

Crook looked unperturbed. "You don't have to. We aim to please. I'll be in touch," he added, looking around for the bowler and ulster he had discarded on arrival. "If any more doctors, spurious or the genuine article, should give you a tinkle . . ."

"There have been too many doctors in this case already," retorted Doreen in her crispest voice. "Aunt Abby wouldn't have approved. She used to say too many doctors filled the church-yard."

"Everything you tell me about her makes me wish more and more I'd had a chance of meeting her in the flesh," said Mr. Crook wistfully. "Of course, that could be rectified hereafter, but me, I'm like the butterfly." (Doreen broke into an explosive uncontrollable giggle.) "I live for the hour. Be seeing you."

And he was gone.

viii ◇

THE POLICE REQUEST for assistance in the Freda Woods case had not met with any considerable response. Anyone using the lane that night had been asked to get in touch, even if he believed he had no useful information to offer. But nothing of any value had eventuated, the only informants proving to have been either in the wrong place or in the right place at the wrong time. The solitary night bus would have passed Marigold Bottom before the girl could have reached it, assuming that Mrs. Lovibond's evidence was accurate, and there was no reason to suppose that it was not. The police didn't for a moment believe that no other members of the community had passed that way on the Monday evening, but cynically assumed they had their own reasons for not wanting to publicize their actions; one at least must be able to help them to establish the truth about the dead girl, but it was asking more than even the most optimistic copper could hope for to expect him to come forward. Then came the arrest of Frankie Piper and the force breathed again, as nice an open-and-shut case as you could look for—no alibi for Monday night, the girl's pearls in his possession and his fingerprints all over the Poets House. Too good to be true, you might say, and of course it was. Crook had to come pushing his great elephant's trunk into the case and that changed everything. Because everyone in the force knew his reputation; it was commonly believed that if he couldn't rake up the evidence to get his man off the hook he'd sit up of nights like the lady with her embroidery frame spinning the right pattern. "Here we go," groaned Mount. And off they went.

Crook was still occupying his room at Mrs. Fred's, and running up what seemed to her a criminally large telephone bill between himself and London.

"A good thing no one thought of rationing speech," she remarked to her husband. "Got a tongue like the clapper of a bell working overtime."

"There's a man's life at stake, even if we don't top them any more," Fred reminded her soberly.

But he wasn't the only one to be impressed. There were, in fact, some who might have helped the authorities, none of whom had surfaced, each for his own reasons. But when Crook's name became freely associated with the Piper defense, one of them reluctantly made a move.

"Gentleman on the telephone for you, Mr. Crook," said Mrs. Fred. "Said you wouldn't know the name."

"If he won't give it I'll never know, will I?" said Crook genially.

"Something to do with Frankie Piper, he said."

The anonymous caller, sounding apprehensive, told Crook, "I believe I may have some information that would interest you about this girl they found in the wood."

"How much?" asked Crook bluntly, and he heard a whistle of indignation at the other end of the line. "How much information," Crook explained in bland tones.

"It might be enough to get your man the benefit of the doubt. I know you have a big reputation in the south of England," he added.

"That's right," Crook agreed without a shadow of vanity. "Everyone knows about me, particularly the slops. Mind you, they know most of it wrong, but who cares?"

"As a matter of fact," the rather desperate voice continued, "I'd like your advice—I'm in rather an awkward situation."

"That makes three of you," Crook agreed. "You and Frankie Piper and the chap responsible. Unless you were going to tell me . . ."

"That I know who did it? Of course not. In that case I'd have gone to the police direct, wouldn't I?"

"Well, I don't know, do I?" returned Crook sensibly. "Meaning you haven't?"

"Meaning I haven't. I can't tell you who was responsible or even if the chap was involved, only . . ."

"Oh, brother!" whispered Crook. "You must like trouble. Now remember the one about walls having ears, and it's never truer than when you're on the blower. So—roll out the barrel and you'll find me waiting to do the honors and the sooner the better. Where are you speaking from, by the way?"

"I'm in a call box," said the voice.

"Very sensible," agreed Crook heartily. "That way they can't trace your call, and anteaters have nothing on the police when it comes to long noses."

His visitor arrived shortly afterward. He was one of those solid yet somehow unnoticeable men whose strength, if they should opt for crime, lies in their very lack of individuality. You could pass him a dozen times in the street and not recognize him on the thirteenth occasion.

"Wasted on an honest life," Crook used to mourn.

"As I told you I want your advice as much as anything," the stranger said, feeling in his waistcoat pocket for a visiting card that he handed across the table.

Crook looked at it. Dr. Charles Gray. "Well, blow me down!" said Crook.

"It's genuine," said the man sharply. "I am a doctor."

"Know those old maps?" Crook asked. "Where there's a section labeled Here Be Dragons? This case is a bit like that—Here Be Doctors. They're like the oysters—thick and fast they came at last—if you are the last of them, that is. Dr. Glass, the police doctor, the mysterious doctor on the line, now you."

"I suppose you're wondering why I didn't come forward before," suggested Gray abruptly.

"I never wonder why chaps don't want to tangle with the police. No legal beagle of your own?"

"I wasn't aware I was going to need one, and in any case I've none I'd care to consult in the circumstances. And to be frank with you, if I hadn't heard you were working on the case I probably wouldn't have come forward now. But as I say, I know your reputation, and I can't believe you'd be acting for Piper if you hadn't good reason to suppose him innocent."

"Best of all reasons," beamed Crook. "He's my client. Well now, let's start. Anything you can tell me gratefully received, no matter how insignificant it may appear to you. It never does to forget that even little fish are sweet."

"I've no evidence to support your contention," the doctor pointed out in his rather stiff way. "I didn't see anyone that night, not Piper or anyone else, but I can testify that there was someone else in the lane at approximately the right time and in the right place."

"Heaven's gift to the sleuth," Crook agreed. "Someone beside yourself, you mean, of course." He looked like an outsized weasel who has just espied a particularly succulent bunny.

"Naturally that's what I mean. And if you're going to ask me why I didn't go to the police in the first place, well, I'd no real evidence that they could accept and I could be getting an innocent man into trouble. Then when they arrested Piper, I was glad I'd held my peace, the case against him seems unshakable. And I still may be making trouble for a man who never set eyes on the girl, which is why I'd rather come to you . . ."

"I get you," said Crook patiently. "You said you didn't see anyone?"

"I saw his transport, and that should be simple to identify."

"Now we're going places. How simple?"

"It was a lorry, carrying fruit and vegetables, presumably to Brendan Market. Not many of the lorries use Falcon Lane, come to that I don't use it myself three times a year, and if it hadn't been for the unusual circumstances . . ."

"That you're going to explain to me?" offered Crook. He had heard that cats always take the longest way around, whereas dogs have an uneering nose for the short cut, but there are still people who prefer cats.

"As I've said, I'm a doctor and my particular interest is in the field of maternity cases, though naturally I have a general practice. That night I was out on a late call, a patient was giving birth prematurely, there was hemorrhaging, I needn't go into details, but it was a touch-and-go affair, and unfortunately in this case it was go. That is, I was able to save the child but I lost the mother. Don't think I'm blaming myself, I don't believe anyone

could have saved her, it was a miracle that the child survived.
The husband, who was at the hospital, went almost berserk. I
believe he'd have attacked me if we'd been alone. If I could only
save one, he stormed, why didn't I save his wife? I'm not God, I
told him, I did what I could. Eventually we had to sedate him, he
wouldn't look at the child—we could get it adopted, smothered,
anything. It was a trying evening."

"That sounds like the understatement of the year," said Crook
respectfully. "So?"

"I'm telling you all this to explain why I was taking the lane
that night instead of sticking to the High Road, which I should
normally have done. There's always a fair amount of night traffic
going that way, and I hadn't been long on it when I heard someone yelling, another driver, and after a moment I realized he was
addressing himself to me.

" 'If you want to commit suicide there are better ways of doing
it,' the chap was shouting. 'Me, I aim to arrive in one piece.' I was
staggered. The chap went on, 'I've been watching you, serve you
right if I was to report you. Chaps like you shouldn't be given a
license, drunk as an owl that's what you are.' That's when I
realized I was weaving all over the road. I've been driving for
twenty-five years and never had my license endorsed," added the
doctor grimly. "And it's not that there was anything wrong with
the car, I was the one who was out of control. I couldn't get that
hospital scene out of my head. Not the father so much as the
child. Perhaps I should tell you that I lost my own wife in child-
birth twenty years ago. They say time heals everything, it's not
true. Anyway, I thought the sooner I got away from the mainstream into some side lane, where I couldn't make trouble for
myself or anyone else, the better. So when we reached the lane a
minute or so later I turned in, hoping the chap had better things
to do than take my number and report me. Mind you, I didn't
think he would, but you can't stop on that main road and it
seemed to me the best thing I could do was to remove myself
from the danger area."

"A pity all drivers who're a bit under the weather don't have
your good sense," Crook assured him.

"I knew about the lane's reputation, but I didn't take that too seriously, either. I hadn't gone very far, only about a mile, when I conked out."

Crook raised his big red eyebrows. "I thought you implied she was running as sweet as a nut."

"I said I conked out, not the car. As a rule doctors get used to tragedy, it's part of the warp and woof of their experience, and you have to accept your own along with everyone else's, but that night seemed different. It had been a hard day even before this last case, and I was only just up after an attack of flu. Anyway, I decided to stop for a few minutes and have a cigarette, so I drew into the side of the road—it was pretty dark, they don't light the lane much—and got out my case. Everything was dead quiet, no traffic at all. I didn't even hear any of the night birds calling or any animals on the move."

"It's a lane, not a jungle," Crook protested.

"There's a lot of life in the country at night. You're a towns-man— Well, as I say, I got out my cigarettes, and then I found my lighter wasn't functioning, and I don't carry matches. It seemed the last straw. I felt I needed that smoke as a suffocating person needs oxygen. I waited for a few minutes, no one came, so I drove on hoping someone would overtake me. And round the next corner I saw this lorry, drawn up in the middle of the road, lights blazing. Another chap wanting a quiet fag, I thought, but then I realized the driver was missing. Naturally, I supposed he'd felt the call of nature and gone into the bushes—there was a hedge on either side, pretty tall at that—so I drew up behind him and waited. Well, Mr. Crook, I waited a pretty long time. In fact, I began to get suspicious."

"Howzat?" asked Mr. Crook, in a manner that wouldn't have disgraced Lord's Cricket Ground.

"I told you the lane has a bad name—there have been some nasty holdups and at least one death for which no one has been called to account. An elderly man practically cut to pieces with bicycle chains, and by what the police could learn, it was for less than a five-pound note."

"And you thought someone had collared the driver? What was the lorry carrying?"

"Ostensibly fruit and vegetables. But there was no knowing what else could have been on board."

"You think the driver had been hi-jacked?" Crook looked puzzled.

"I thought it might be part of a plot, and the driver had made himself scarce on purpose. And if you think that's melodramatic . . ."

"I wouldn't give much for a world where nothing melodramatic ever happened," Crook assured him. He wished he could put in something about charging by time, only now he was on the receiving end, and patience is a virtue, et cetera. "What did you have in mind? Drugs among the Brussels sprouts?" Drugs were in the news just then, but Crook couldn't remember a time when they hadn't been. He remembered stories of playing cards changing hands in the night clubs that sprang up after the World War One, with cocaine concealed in the backs.

"I didn't work it out," Gray admitted. "It just seemed to me a pretty fishy situation, and my best bet might be to make myself scarce. So I edged past the lorry and drove home. It's an odd thing," he added, "but the incident so impressed me it had the same therapeutic effect as a cigarette might have done. Anyhow, by the time I rejoined the mainstream of traffic I was as steady as any driver needs to be. I glanced at the paper next morning but there was nothing about a lorry being mixed up in a raid, and I put the matter out of my mind."

"Till you heard about the girl being found in the wood. It was nearby?"

"The lorry was parked by Marigold Bottom. Naturally I started adding two and two. Still, I hadn't set eyes on a driver, I couldn't swear he'd been within earshot and I didn't hear a sound, which was strange if there was a struggle going on on the other side of the hedge."

"According to my reading of it the struggle was practically nil," Crook reminded him. "She wasn't strangled, she was suffocated, and the police wallah thought it wasn't premeditated. Just her bad luck that she was in the wrong place at the right time."

"I was still uncertain what to do—there was this other lorry driver who might remember what my car was like and might even support his contention that I was drunk at the wheel of a car when I realized the police were tying up the two deaths, this girl and the old woman from the Poets House. It seemed to me highly improbable, to put it mildly, that a lorry driver would have been able to work all that out—telephone the niece and pass himself off as a doctor . . ."

"It 'ud depend on the lorry driver," Crook reminded him. "When I was a lad they were all cloth caps and mufflers, but we're all cultured fellows now. You ask the chaps in the know who buy the transistors and the Leica cameras—it's not the professors or the clergy; it's probably not even you or me. Still, if your driver can show he got to the market at the usual time or near it, he should be in the clear. Happen to notice the name on the lorry?"

"Well, I did. It was Moss of Ferndown Green. As you say, this man can probably clear himself of any connection with Mrs. Nicholas's death, which puts him out of it. It seemed to me, though, that my evidence, if that's the word, could get your man the benefit of the doubt. The finding of the necklace was pretty damning, I thought—in fact, until I heard your name in connection with the case it didn't occur to me that Piper wasn't guilty . . ."

"He can't have been guilty," interposed Crook. "He wasn't there that night."

"You mean that's what he says—and you believe him."

"I wouldn't be acting for him if I didn't, would I?"

"It's an odd story," the doctor persisted.

"Not the only one. As for the benefit of the doubt, I never saw that was so much of a benefit as the pundits try to tell me. To spend the rest of your life being pointed at as one of the lucky chaps who got away with murder. Besides, there's a little girl— you know how cruel kids can be to each other: 'Look, there goes Vicky Piper, her daddy's a murderer. Why didn't he hang then? (Or rot in prison, it comes to much the same thing.) Because clever Mr. Crook got him off. Did it cost an awful lot?' No, I think I must do a bit better for Frankie than that. Mind you, it's not my job to name the real criminal, that's for the police, only sometimes you have to oblige the rozzers to clear your own client."

"You don't sound as though you cared much for the police," murmured Dr. Gray.

"I love them just the same way they love me, like a brother. Only some brothers you like better than others. Come to that, you ain't going to be their favorite man when the balloon goes up."

"I told you I wanted your advice. If I were to go to them now, would it help Piper?"

"I'll tell you who it might help, and that's the chap who's really responsible. No, the fact is that so long as the police have got their man, or so they believe, he'll start thinking he's safe, and that's when they start making trouble for themselves."

"I won't conceal the fact that I have my own reputation in mind," the doctor confessed. "Doctors are like parsons, can't afford the smallest blot on the 'scutcheon. Particularly if— Are you a married man, Mr. Crook?"

The lawyer shook his head. "I count my blessings," he said piously.

"An unmarried doctor is like an unmarried parson—he's a natural suspect. People seem to think he owes it to his profession not to be single. Not that I'm not a married man in a sense," he added, "but it was all over before I settled here, and probably no one knows . . . And I believe I have a vocation, if that doesn't sound too smug. I'm not like most men who have a number of strings to their bow, of which their work is one. My work is my life, and if anything happened to interrupt that, it would be like a death sentence to me. And even the fact of a policeman calling at your house starts tongues wagging. You can say you were helping them in their inquiries, but everyone knows what that means. The men who are at the local station assisting usually stay there later."

"I get you," Crook agreed. "Well?"

"I have a number of policemen and their families on my register," Gray went on. "I know they're the last people to make rash accusations they can't support with cut-and-dried evidence. They can't afford to make mistakes, any more than doctors can, not just as individuals but as an organization. There's greater faith in the police force of this country than anywhere in the world. And the case against Piper is pretty strong. After all, he had a motive—if the girl recognized him . . ."

"You think she'd have gone legging it to the police? We don't know that she particularly wanted to attract attention. She'd made off with Mummy's pearls, and though Mrs. Christmas wouldn't have brought an action—in a sense you could say she asked for what happened to her, like those old women who yell blue murder when they wake up and find a burglar on the premises, and blue murder is how it ends, though the intruder may never have intended violence. The way I read it is that X wanted to shut her mouth and shut it a bit more effectually than he intended. Any good counsel could have got him a verdict of manslaughter, but assuming he's someone who can't afford to go to the police— You know," he added, "with local feeling being the way it is, young Frankie's probably as well off in police hands as he could be anywhere."

"I'm not so concerned with him," said the doctor bluntly. "He's got you on his side. This driver's another matter, and the fact that he was on the spot doesn't prove anything. I was on the spot, and I can't tell the police what happened. After all, one needs a motive—and Piper had that."

"There's usually a motive for murder unless you're dealing with a raging lunatic," Crook reminded him. "This girl may have seen something, or someone, and started to raise Cain. I'll still ask a few questions about the driver. Suppose the rozzers are barking up the wrong tree and the two crimes ain't connected . . ."

"It's a bad bargain in any case," the doctor insisted. "A neurotic adolescent and a diseased old woman, put together they don't add up to a healthy member of the community. One of these days they'll start rationing time; it'll be our only hope unless we're to have mass immigrations to other planets—this globe can't afford to support useless lives. I tell you, Mr. Crook, I've known colleagues sit up all night with patients who're no more than synthetic bodies just able to breathe."

"But it's your profession that's responsible," Crook agreed. "When I was a boy there were known killers of the old and the diseased. Well, you've changed all that, we're carrying the burden now—it's a case of heads they win and tails we lose. You know," he added, going off at a tangent, "it's a good thing the twelve apostles weren't policemen. I mean, you show me a rozzer who'll take anything on faith—like your story or this driver's when we have it—and I'll eat my Sunday-go-to-meeting titfer. Like I said, you're not going to be their favorite man, but then"—he grinned reassuringly—"you'll be in good company."

He caught sight of himself in the glass as he spoke, the comfortably rotund figure in its appalling red-brown suit. "They'd all put their hands in their pockets and subscribe for a wreath if they heard I'd handed in my dinner pail." He refrained from adding the slanderous suggestion that there might be some who wouldn't be above giving fate a hand in shoving him underground.

"Know something?" said Dr. Gray, rising to go. "If I'd been that old king, Canute was the name, and you'd sat on the shore and told me to retreat, I'd have gone back so fast you'd have thought you were in the Gobi Desert."

Crook looked honestly delighted. "No one can say fairer than that," he admitted. "Here, you better take my phone number, Mrs. Fred will take a message if I'm out. But I'll pass on the hint I give on all these occasions, the one about silence being golden, and gold was never much more valuable than it is now." He remembered as a small boy that gold had been quite casually exchanged over grocer's counters or handed to the chap who came for the rent, but he refrained from saying anything, there was no sense dating yourself beyond recall, even if you were believed, and quite a lot of people simply didn't believe it.

That's a turn-up for the book, he reflected when his visitor had gone. And it was to be hoped the doctor wasn't doing any delicate operations that morning, you could hardly blame him if his hand was a bit shaky. Of course, a righteous man would probably have told him about his civic duty—but I'm a breadwinner not a parson, Crook reminded himself, and if he walked in and said he'd done for the girl himself they'd probably only have told him he was the two hundred and eightieth on the list. Funny how chaps liked to confess to murders they couldn't conceivably have committed.

A case of conscience? Crook wondered. Whatever he came for, it wasn't for fun, but it's the first—no, the second—stroke of luck Frankie's had.

The first, of course, was having a wife like Ann who had the sense to pull Crook into the picture.

ix

CROOK HAD HIS OWN WAYS of getting information. For all his odd appearance, he was like another winner, the Pied Piper of Hamelin, who lured away an army, first of rats and then of children, and none could say him nay. Within twenty-four hours of the doctor's visit Crook knew more about Mr. Moss, the owner of the lorry the doctor had seen in Falcon Lane on the fatal Monday night, than most of that worthy's neighbors.

For one thing, he realized why the driver was keeping his trap shut, even though he might know nothing about the dead girl. Mr. Moss was a mean-featured little man with a mind to match. He cherished a conviction that the whole of society was in a conspiracy to do him down; he trusted no one. Not his wife—and how right he was there, she'd gone off with another fellow years before—not his competitors, not his business associates, and certainly not his driver of the moment, Terry Lamb. So why keep Terry on, you might ask. The answer was twofold. In the first place he found it very difficult to keep staff. Chaps didn't have to queue up as they'd done when he was a young man, to get something to put on their backs and in their bellies; nowadays they could pick and choose, particularly when they were as knowledgeable as Terry was. A bit of a wild chap, perhaps, but he could use his wits, knew providence had given him feet for more than standing on, and the worst mark against him was a tendency to change jobs when they ceased to interest him. "Have to settle down one of these days," he would explain. "Make the most of your liberty." His had virtually come to an end the day he set eyes on old Moss's daughter, Sally. Up till that time the boot had been on the other foot. Girls were a pushover for Terry

113

Lamb, and what was there so special about this ardent scornful stuck-up little redhead—that's what he asked himself—to change him as suddenly as the toad in the fairy tale was changed into a prince? Because he hadn't intended to work for this old misery, not likely, and he was just going to tell Moss so when the old fellow said, "My daughter is my partner. When I'm not available you'll take your orders from her."

"That'll be the day," said Terry. He could imagine what this sour-faced old sod's daughter would be like—and then the door opened and Sally came in. Take her features apart and she was no beauty—not a patch really on Lila or June or Gwendoline—a little bit of a thing not much taller than a candleflame and oddly enough making him think of one. She had stood on the threshold, looking questioningly from one man to the other.

"This is Lamb," said the old man shortly. "The new driver."

And Terry, who'd have hooted at the notion that he could be manipulated like this (though, mark you, the wages were slightly above average and that was suspicious in itself) not a minute before, heard himself inquire meekly, "When would you like me to start, Mr. Moss?"

"Where did you find Adonis?" Sally asked her father when Terry had gone.

Old Moss looked up, startled. "Don't start getting any funny ideas in that direction, my girl. That chap's my new driver—just that. Nothing more."

"I bet he doesn't think so," retorted Sally, undaunted.

"You're my daughter and one day this business will be yours. I haven't worked fourteen hours a day most of my life for the benefit of a layabout like young Lamb."

"If you think he's like that, I wonder at you hiring him at all."

"He'll do for a fill-gap. I know his type, they never stay the course, but the lorry won't drive itself. That chap's had more girls than you've had hot dinners," he added warningly.

"You're always on about the value of experience," said Sally.

All the same, when the situation developed and she told him

calmly that she was in love and they were going to get married,
his first impulse was to give Terry his cards.

"Up to you," Sally said, "but if Terry goes I go with him."

He couldn't believe his ears. She was the only thing in his life
he didn't evaluate in terms of pounds, shillings and pence.

"You're not twenty-one, my girl," he reminded her.

"That's why we're waiting till the autumn. Give you a bit of
time to think things over."

"Any notion what you're going to live on as Lamb's wife?"

"What my husband can earn, of course. And you don't have to
worry. Terry's not going to be any man's legman for long. Moss
and Lamb. Or perhaps Lamb and Moss. Or just Terence Lamb."

Crook didn't pick all this up overnight, of course, but he didn't
waste much time seeing how the land lay. There's no place like a
pub for getting information and he hung around the bar of the
Rocking Horse Inn, not pushing himself, you understand, but not
letting himself be overlooked either. It was sometimes said of him
that he had ears an elephant might envy, and he worked them
overtime. He learned quite a lot about Terry, too, enough to
realize that if he had offered the wretched Freda a lift, got a bit
fresh—because he was playing his cards very carefully where
Sally was concerned and patience wasn't one of his strong suit—
well, say he had done just that thing, got a bit fresh and suddenly
found himself in bad trouble, he wasn't the sort who'd come
forward to ease things for a chap who should know enough to
stand on his own plates of meat. Sir Galahad was a nice chap, but
he's been dead a long time, and there was only one Galahad in
the whole setup at the Round Table.

So not much later, when he came whistling up the High Road
to turn into Falcon Lane, Terry was surprised to see a big yellow
car drawn up just inside the entrance, and a chap who'd convert
you to Darwin's theory of evolution, which says we've all sprung
from apes and some not so far as others, poking about in the
hood. His first inclination was to lean out of the cab and offer his
assistance. He was a natural mechanic and there was plenty to be
made that way these days, but he couldn't stand being shut up in
a workshop all day, clock on, clock off, yes, sir, no, sir, three

bags full—the driving really suited him better, though he had too much sense, where this particular employer was concerned, to get involved in any little profitable games on the side. Anyway, this setup could well be a trap—and nothing to do with Freda Woods at that. When he got down to help this great ginger-colored type, two more might emerge from behind the hedge, and he'd had some experience of what a bicycle chain can do to an unarmed man. Besides, he owed it to Sally to stay in one piece till October, to say nothing of the fact that the last thing he wanted was to call attention to himself at this juncture. So far no one had approached him about the events of that Monday night, and that's the way he wanted to keep it. He probably wouldn't have recognized Galahad's name if he'd heard it—what's that, a horse? he'd say—and there'd been no witnesses so far as he knew, or none prepared to come forward. There'd been the fellow on the motorbike, of course, but he'd gone by like the wind, and doubtless had his own reasons for not wanting the police to know his whereabouts that evening. What folk don't know can't hurt 'em, he reminded himself, inaccurately, as it happened. So "Sod the old so-and-so," he murmured, and stamping on the accelerator, he went past like the Wrath of God.

When the lorry was a convenient distance along the lane, Mr. Crook coolly readjusted a couple of wires he'd thoughtfully transposed to lend verisimilitude to his act, and got back into the driving seat. He hadn't a doubt that this was the lorry Dr. Gray had seen and the man at the wheel the driver whom he hadn't. Enter the invisible man, said Mr. Crook in his melodramatic way, following fast. It wasn't long before, rounding a corner, he caught sight of the lorry again. Not that he'd had any fear of losing it, you wouldn't have persuaded him that the Superb couldn't have won the Le Mans contest if she'd put her mind to it. But it did occur to him that the driver had slowed his pace. Did he, wondered Crook, suspect something? And, if so, was he waiting for a chance to let the smaller vehicle go by and then engineer a crash? It wouldn't be the first time something of the kind had occurred, and there'd be no witnesses.. The doctor had been telling the truth when he declared that not many people used the lane after dark. Of course, those

who normally used it might be showing their good sense by staying away just now so as not to attract attention; though, since the
police had got their man, this seemed unnecessarily cautious. But
then they know I'm on the trail, Crook reminded himself, and
only a mug plays with fire. Having an unquenchable predeliction
for staying alive as long as possible, Mr. Crook prudently slowed
his pace also.

At the wheel of the lorry Terry Lamb was troubled. A man
used to noticing details, he had realized that the yellow car didn't
carry local number plates, and more than that, he didn't normally
travel this way. More than ever he was convinced that the inspec-
tion of the hood had been a bit of not very subtle camouflage. So
he slowed a bit to let the fellow go by, and his suspicions were
reinforced when the big car didn't pass him. He put on speed
again, looking in his driving mirror, and sure enough there it
came, following him step by step, like the fearful fiend in the
kid's poem. Suddenly the end of the lane came in sight, and he
leaped ahead, making the turn so abruptly that only his skill
avoided a collision with another lorry on the main road.

"Why don't you keep it for the circus?" the driver yelled, then
he saw the man at the wheel and grinned. "You'll have both our
heads rolling one of these days," he threatened.

"You'll never notice the difference, mate," Terry yelled back.
A new spirit infused his voice, because his mirror showed him
that the grotesque yellow car had turned right and was now
battling with the oncoming stream of lorries all making for Joe's
caff, where they'd stop for a quarter of an hour for a cuppa and a
doorstep. "Happy dreams, chum," he said under his breath. "You
can't put yourself under one of their wheels too soon for me."

Crook drove steadily for a short distance, then took advantage
of a break in the traffic to perform a U-turn, and started to
come back. Now he was mingled with the train of lorries and the
occasional private car. Quite soon he realized the lorries were all
stopping and he saw the reason why. He knew the rules about
cafés like this one, as exclusive as the clubs old buffers used to
belong to in the days of privilege. He had too much sense to

expect service here, though he appreciated the type of fare Joe provided—sandwiches, almost solid enough to stand on, potato crisps, meat pies and a hearty sort of cake decorated with wisps of coconut that he recalled from the coffee-stall days of his youth at Hyde Park Corner and in the Fulham Road. No license, of course, but then the authorities wouldn't want to encourage men to drink when they were on the road, particularly seeing the value of the cargo some of them carried. There'd be special arrangements made for them when they'd delivered their goods. So it never occurred to him to try and muscle in, not even when he saw the lorry with MOSS on the side standing as untenanted as it must have done when Dr. Gray caught up with it. Terry himself was standing at the counter talking to Joe. Still, he (Crook) hadn't come all this way for nothing, so, oblivious to the hostile and curious stares of some of the drivers, he hopped out of the Superb and marched up to the counter.

"Began to think Daisy must have broken down again," Joe was saying. "Not like you to let the young chaps beat you to it, and anyway I don't like to miss my regulars even for one night." He turned and favored Crook with a wordless stare.

"On the right road for Brudding?" Mr. Crook inquired. "Some joker's taken down the sign at the crossroads."

"Right ahead," said Joe. "Turn left at the church and over the level crossing."

"Ta a million," said Crook, speaking as though Terry didn't exist. He got back into the Superb and drove off. Very interesting, he gloated.

The drivers were slamming down their mugs, cramming the last morsel of food into their mouths, lighting up their fags and getting back on the job. Mr. Crook, who was in no hurry, let a number of them go past him. He was waiting for Terry to take off, so he tooled briskly around the first bend and then dropped to a snail's pace, his ears out for the sound of the lorry's engine. He hadn't come this far to be run down now.

He had to wait quite a while. Back at the caff Terry ordered another sandwich that he didn't want, while Joe looked at him curiously, wondering what was in the wind. In a job like this you got to know chaps pretty well, their behavior mostly followed a certain pattern according to their temperament, when it differentiated you could be pretty sure something was blowing up. Terry's usual program was first in, first out, so when he came trailing behind a line of normal latecomers and didn't seem in a hurry even now, you could tell yourself he had something on his mind. Terry waited till the coast was pretty clear, then he said, "That chap in the yellow Rolls, the one who asked the way to Brudding—what's he want in a place like Brudding this time of night? It's lights out by ten for everyone there."

Joe looked surprised. "Well, I don't know, do I? What's it matter anyway? I'm not his guardian angel."

"He was mucking about with that car of his—and what museum did he rob to lay hands on her?—at the far end of Falcon Lane when I came through," said Terry in gloomy tones. "Ever come this way before?"

"Not that I recall," acknowledged Joe.

"And he turned right at the end of the lane, so what's he doing here?"

"You had your chance to ask him," Joe pointed out. "Still, tourist likely, doesn't know his way around."

"Funny time of night for a tourist to be out on his owney-oh."

"Oh well!" Joe shrugged. The gesture and the tone of his voice suggested that he was referring to a lower order of humanity. A new thought struck him. "You don't think he's police or anything?"

"No skin off my nose if he is. Oh well, time I was on my way." He climbed back into the cab of the lorry and started her off in a way that made Joe raise his eyebrows.

"Lucky for you she's as strong as an ox," he offered.

"More like a pregnant cow," said Terry inelegantly. "Look at the way she broke down the other night, nearly landed me in Queer Street. Not that it's any use saying anything to old Mossbanks about her. It's the driver's fault, the road's fault, the weather, Act of God. Nothing's ever wrong with Daisy. I believe he thinks almost as much of her as he does of Sally."

"Mean to say you didn't even mention about the breakdown?"

"I told you, it's a waste of breath. Mind you, Sally's always on at me to insist on a new lorry, but then you haven't met the old man."

"Your Sally sounds as if she had a lot of sense. You should listen to her sometime."

"No sense giving them their head before they've got the ring on their finger," retorted Terry, and off he roared.

What's biting him? Joe wondered. Not like Terry Lamb to worry about anyone except Terry, and now Sally presumably. Worked things out very nicely for himself by all accounts—old Moss would cut up warm and Sally was his only child. It 'ud pay young Terry to keep his nose clean a while longer. Joe looked up and down the road. There'd be a bit more casual custom, most of the regulars had gone through, then he could start packing up for the night. He didn't think about Crook again, except to wonder why Terry should take him so seriously. Unless, of course, the young fool had been mucking about with the stranger's wife, only surely with a wedding in October, and a nice warm father-in-law—well, warm anyway—he wouldn't be taking any chances. Though he hadn't reckoned to notice the stranger particularly, he realized at this juncture that he'd as soon face a charging rhino as Crook on the warpath. Which was rum, considering the chap had hardly opened his mouth and hadn't even looked at Terry Lamb. Joe glanced at his watch, then up and down the road. Dead empty and that's how it 'ud stay till some of the chaps started coming home. They'd have their fill at the Blue Rabbit at Brendan, where special arrangements were made for them, and back they'd go, like a lot of overweight swallows skimming the tarmac ...

He started to pack up the crockery when he saw something coming back down the road, and blow him down, if it wasn't the spectacular yellow car with old Mr. Magoo in person at the wheel. The Superb reached the coffee stall and stopped. Crook got out.

"Lost your way?" asked Joe civilly. "No, don't tell me. There's been an earthquake and Brudding's disappeared." And he added, "I'm just closing up. Anyway, this is a drivers' caff, we don't serve anyone outside the trade."

"I don't go much for the soft stuff myself," Mr. Crook acknowledged. "That chap, Lamb, the one who works for Moss, comes through here most nights, doesn't he?"

"If you're acting for the police," said Joe, "you ought to show me your warrant."

"Whatever put that idea into your head?" inquired Crook. "You surprise me, honest you do, though not so much as you'd surprise them. Obliged if you'd give him a message," he went on, putting his hand in his pocket and hauling out a card. "Crook's the name, Arthur Crook. The Golden Goose 'ull find me and Mrs. Fred 'ull take a message if I'm out." He uncapped a pen and scrawled the telephone number across the top of the card. "Sooner me than the police," he added explanatorily. "At least, that's the way I'd see it."

He saw that his name hadn't created a dent here, but it didn't bother him. "I might have stopped him tonight," he added, putting his pen back in his pocket, "only you can't interfere with a chap when he's on the job, can you?" He was perfectly sincere in that. To him there was nothing on earth so important as work. "It's about that night he didn't show up here," he went on chattily. "Thought he might be able to help me in some inquiries I'm making."

Joe looked at the card in his hand. It might have been written in Sanskrit for all the sense it made to him.

"Who says he'd want to get mixed up in that?" he demanded.

"He'd want to see right done, wouldn't he? A Monday, wasn't it? The night he had trouble with Mr. Moss's van?"

Joe stiffened and the angry color came into his face. "So that's the game? Old Moss employing spies, is he? Well, I wouldn't put it past him. But you've come to the wrong shop, mister."

"Never met Mr. Moss," Crook assured him placidly. "Hard case, from all accounts. That's why I thought Terry and me might have a bit of a natter on the quiet. Up to him, of course. Only when you're looking for needles in a haystack you don't have to keep your peepers out for a darner. Even a little one can help."

"And Terry Lamb's your needle?"

"Could be. Mind you, he's free to refuse. Up to him. Only there's some chances even a chap like that doesn't care to take. Ta a million. Of course," he added, turning back, as an afterthought, "could be he could clear everything up on the blower. Wouldn't want to take up his spare time, only—I have a living to get, too."

"I'll say," agreed Joe. "Where'd you find her?" He indicated the Superb.

Crook beamed. "You could call it a natural affinity. Don't forget my message, will you?" And without giving Joe a chance to reply, he was back at the wheel and streaming down the road like the morning light.

The next morning he told Mrs. Fred he'd got to go to London for a day or two. "Can't butter my bread with one fishball," he explained in his oracular way. But he arranged to keep on the room and paid his scot in advance. "Anybody rings up, get the message," he coaxed, with a grin as ingratiating as that of a full-grown alligator. "I'll be up to collect Friday."

"Anything to do with this poor girl, Mr. Crook?" coaxed Mrs. Fred in her turn.

"Well, everything I do here has to do with her in a way," Crook allowed cautiously. "Had a notion this chap might be able to help. Of course, if he don't ring . . ." He shrugged, but he hadn't any doubts in his own mind. Terry would come through all right, and he knew from years of experience that his own best bet was to be mysteriously unavailable for twenty-four hours at least. That 'ud make the young fellow curious, and curiosity has killed more than cats.

"He's a sudden sort of gentleman, isn't he?" commented P. C. Doyle in his sedate way when he came into the Golden Goose that night and heard that Crook had vanished London-ward. "Here today and gone tomorrow . . ."

"But back the day after," put in Fred. "Leastways, that's what he told Beattie. And the room's paid for in advance."

"I'll tell you this," said P. C. Doyle in the tone of a man who knows the whereabouts of the lost gold of the Incas and has resolved to share his secret with his best friend, "I'd sooner have that Inspector Mount and his sergeant on my tail than Mr. Crook. I wonder who it is he has in mind," he added reflectively. But no one was able to enlighten him.

"He's like that bedbug we used to hear about when we were

kids," Fred acknowledged, "the one that had no wings at all but got there just the same."

P. C. Doyle thoughtfully rubbed his arm. "Makes me itch just to think of it," he said.

Terry got the message from Joe when he came through the following night, and instantly suspicion blazed up in him like a brushwood heap when someone throws down a careless match.

"Who is this flaming Crook?" he demanded. "Never heard of him."

"Seems to know about you," retorted Joe. "Got the idea you might be able to help him."

"He's got a hope," said Terry, throwing down the card.

"I did think it might be your boss, but he says he's never met him. Wouldn't put it past him, though . . ."

Terry's head came up with a jerk. "What's that supposed to mean?"

"It means he's the sort of chap who's used to getting his own way. You in a jam, Terry?"

Terry shook his head. "Not that I know." He picked up the card that he had indignantly tossed down. "Arthur Crook . . ." he repeated.

"You must be in the cart," said another voice, and he turned sharply to see a driver called Williams standing grinning at his elbow. "You only get that chap in when you're—what's the expression?—*in extremis*."

Terry scowled. Williams was a comparative newcomer, a southerner, a foreigner, in short. "Know him, do you?"

"Everybody in London knows him. I did hear he was acting for this Piper chap. You know, the one they think killed the girl in the wood."

"That one?" Terry wondered if he looked as shaken as he felt. "What the hell does he suppose I can do?"

"He's waiting to tell you. Come by Falcon Lane, don't you?"

"That doesn't say I saw her. Anyway, how'd he know?"

"Trust Crook to know a thing like that." Williams grinned again. "Probably been down asking every perishing buttercup if they saw anyone."

"If I'd known anything I'd have gone to the police, wouldn't I?" Terry sounded belligerent.

Williams winked at the assembled company. "Would you, boy? We're not that fond of the police where I come from."

"Have your reasons, I daresay," Terry snapped. "Oh well." He slipped the card into his pocket. "May as well stop him wetting his pants."

Joe looked up. "Take a tip, Terry," he said. "If you were thinking of going to see this Mr. Crook, leave your gun at home."

"I don't know who Mr. Crook thinks will ring him up here," announced Mrs. Fred to her husband. "Unless it's that Inspector Mount, and I did hear they weren't speaking."

"He gets around, does Mr. Crook. You wouldn't believe the number of people have been asking about him." Fred's tone was reverential and somber. "It's not as though he's the kind you'd easy forget."

"Soft," said Mrs. Fred briefly. "All you men are the same. It was the girl got round him. You'd think with her looks and her taking ways she'd have found herself someone better than Frankie Piper."

Fred remembered an orange and white striped dress his wife had insisted on buying the previous summer. To him she'd looked like something off the ice-cream stall, but she couldn't see it. She thought it was sheer Bond Street. Maybe Ann Piper felt the same about Frankie. Love is blind and ought to go around with a guide to keep it out of trouble, but if the plan's ever been tried it hasn't worked. But being a husband of twenty-eight years' standing he prudently held his tongue.

The telephone call came the next day. A voice said, "I have a call for you from London," and Mrs. Fred replied at once, "There's no one from London here."

A voice as unforgettable as its owner broke in like a storm breaking at sea. "There is here, though," it said. "My call come through yet?"

Mrs. Fred told him no.

"It will," prophesied Crook confidently. "When it does say I'll be back in the morning, ten-thirty the Golden Goose." And he rang off. All that fuss, to say nothing of the expense, for a few words you could have put on a postcard, and only a threepenny stamp to pay, reflected frugal Mrs. Fred. That was southerners for you. She frowned her disapproval as she hung up the receiver. The second came within the hour.

"Mr. Crook?" asked a voice she didn't recognize.

"Who wants him?"

"Nosey, aren't you?" said the voice. "I had this message . . ."

"Oh, you!" said Mrs. Fred. "He's just rung from London. Be back tomorrow, Golden Goose, he said, ten-thirty. I suppose he'll know who it is," she added.

"If he doesn't now, he will when I come, won't he?"

And for the second time a telephonic conversation was abruptly closed.

X ❖
❖

EVEN IF HE hadn't seen him at Joe's Café, Crook would have had no difficulty in identifying him when the driver came sauntering into the Golden Goose next morning, a few minutes behind time. That was part of the act, of course. No one was going to hustle Terry Lamb. A lady-killer to his boot straps, Crook decided, and (Crook suspected) no holds barred when it came to dealings with either sex. He lounged in as though he hadn't a care in the world, sent his impudent dark glance around the bar and then moved over to the counter. Crook made no sign of recognition. He'd come over in his own good time, and Crook had never believed in allowing himself to be dominated by a man-made piece of mechanism, like a clock. "Time's there to serve me," he'd say. "When chaps start serving time it's usually on the wrong side of the prison grid."

Up at the counter Terry asked for a pint, but before he'd had time to put down the price the barman observed, "That's Mr. Crook, the gentleman in the brown suit over in the corner."

Terry glanced casually in that direction. "Not likely to mistake him for anyone else," he acknowledged.

"Said he was expecting you," the barman explained, moving to serve a newcomer.

"Never keep a gentleman waiting," Terry agreed, picking up his tankard and moving through the room. Crook watched him come, a tall, athletic young chap, cool as the proverbial cucumber. Terry stopped at his table. "Your name Crook? You wanted a word with me?"

"That was the idea," Crook agreed. "Good of you to turn out."

Terry set down his tankard, pulled out a chair. "I rather got the idea it might be a case of the mountain coming to Mahomet," he explained.

"And you're such a kind-hearted chap you didn't want to shift the mountain." Crook beamed.

"That's one way of putting it. Let's stop arsing about and come down to brass tacks. Joe said something about me being able to help you. He didn't say how."

"He didn't know. Could be you've heard I'm acting for Frankie Piper."

"Frankie . . . ?"

"Oh, come," urged Crook. "No one's that innocent. This chap the police have taken for Freda Woods's death. Now, I know he couldn't have done it . . ."

"Shouldn't you be telling the police, not me?"

"They're such a fussy lot, always asking for proof. A gentleman's word isn't enough for them. No, what I need is evidence."

"What makes you suppose I could give you any?"

"You were in Falcon Lane that night. Oh, I've got a witness to that. That is, he saw your lorry there. Of course, if someone else was driving it . . ."

"That'll be the day," Terry agreed. "Well, what of it? The lorry's there every night. Funny thing," he added, "the police can't think much of your pal's story. They haven't sent me so much as a dicky bird."

"Shocking the way the public won't cooperate," mourned Crook. "My chap hasn't told the police. What do you think of that?"

"More a question of what the police think, I'd have said."

"They must be used to disappointment by this time. Anyway, this chap didn't see why he should get involved. Only when they took an innocent man . . ."

"What makes him so sure Piper is innocent?"

"My clients are always innocent," said Crook impatiently. "Anyway, you're not going to tell me you saw him there."

"I didn't see anyone, except a chap on a motorcycle who went past with the speed of light. And he hadn't got any girl on his pillion and, anyway, it was before we reached Marigold Bottom."

"We?"

"Daisy and me. That's what we call the lorry."

"You didn't approach the police yourself." It was a statement, not a question.

Terry opened his dark eyes. "I couldn't tell them anything. I didn't see the girl, I didn't see anyone who could have killed her. Matter of fact, there's never much traffic in the lane that hour of night."

"Any special reason you shouldn't want anyone to know you were there?" Crook asked.

Terry shot up as if someone had inserted a poker in his spine. "What are you getting at?"

"I was wondering if Mr. Moss knew—that you always take the lane, I mean?"

"Old Mossbags employs me to get his stuff to market on time, it's nothing to him how I get it there."

"I just wondered," soothed Crook.

"And I don't see why I should make the detour and add another fifteen to twenty minutes to my run to oblige a gang of thugs. If they lined up in front of me I'd drive right through them and swear I thought they were ghosts."

"I believe you would at that," Crook acknowledged. "Still, the old man mightn't see it that way. It's a rum thing," he went on, "that you didn't see her, I mean. According to Mrs. Lovibond— that's the one at the Blackbird Café—she'd have been turning into the lane just about the time you were approaching it."

"I don't know how you make that out. Anyway, didn't I read that she was with some chap in a car?"

"If you'll believe that, you'll believe anything. Not her. She was on foot, so how come you didn't see her?"

"You know the lane?" Terry sounded elaborately polite. "The hedges there are pretty high. If she was walking behind them she'd be invisible from the road. And if she had the sense she was born with she wouldn't be on the road. I don't mind telling you I wouldn't care to be about there myself on my tod after dark, not if I was on foot."

"So if you saw a girl on her own you might be tempted to offer her a lift."

"You don't know much about the job, do you, mate?" Terry

suggested. "The bosses are dead nuts against giving lifts. There was a chap called McConnell, he used to use the lane, met a sheilah there one night, regular damsel in distress she was, gave her a lift, well, you know how it is, next night she was there, and by the end of the week she knew about his deliveries—next thing you know they hi-jacked the lorry. If you want my opinion, Mc-Connell was lucky to have a broken thigh and other injuries, kept him in hospital for weeks. Not what I'd choose for myself but better than being in a coffin, which is where his boss would have shoved him if he got the chance. It was after that the other drivers stopped using the lane. They do say the junkies have a hideout there," he added casually.

"Someone should have warned the girl," Crook agreed.

"I don't know what her family was thinking of, letting a kid of sixteen out on her own," declaimed Terry indignantly.

"She was running away from home," Crook reminded him. "Well, you disappoint me, Mr. Lamb. I did hope— You're sure this motorcycling chap couldn't be involved?"

"It could be worse," Terry pointed out. "He might have said he saw your Frankie Piper. That would have scuppered you."

"No, why?" asked Crook, sounding as if he really wanted to know. "I'd simply have realized he was an unreliable witness."

Terry tilted back his chair. "You won't be told, will you?"

"That's my trouble at the moment. No one will tell me anything. Oh, there's Mrs. L. But if you stop to think, the girl had only been in the neighborhood half an hour, we know she was on her own when she left the station, she hadn't had much time to cultivate a boyfriend, and from all accounts she was no Delilah."

"Who's she?" asked Terry.

"A come-up-and-see-me-sometime lady," Crook explained, and Terry laughed shortly. "All the same, it's rum, unless Mrs. Lovibond's got her times wrong, and there's no reason to suppose she has. I mean, the girl couldn't have reached Marigold Bottom on her own feet at the time my witness says he saw your stationary lorry there."

"Look here," exclaimed Terry, "what's this about my lorry?"

Crook explained. "Are you going to tell me it wasn't there?"

"Your pal's got his geography wrong," said Terry coolly. "Oh, I had a breakdown that night all right, but it wasn't anywhere near Marigold Bottom."

"My pal says it was."

"Uses the lane regular, does he?"

"Well, no. This was quite an occasion for him. Feeling a bit under the weather. A doctor," he added. "Had a bad time, baby case."

Terry grinned faintly. "Stopped on to wet the baby's head?" he offered.

"He lost the mother, felt badly about it."

Terry sobered. "Poor bugger!"

"Found he was a bit uncertain in his steering, so turned into the lane and nearly ran kerplump into your lorry jammed right across the road."

"Funny thing I didn't see him," offered Terry.

"According to him, you weren't there."

"Could be right," Terry acknowledged. "I went along to the phone booth to try and get one of the garages to send a man out. No soap, though. All at the bingo, I suppose."

"You mean, no offers?"

"No replies, not so much as a dicky bird. I went back and hung around—thought someone might come along the lane and give me a hand. But—just my luck—no one surfaced. Not even your pal."

"He'd be gone by then. I mean, he hung around Marigold Bottom for a bit . . . waiting for you, see. Wanted a match."

"If you'll believe that you'll believe anything," countered Terry. "I tell you, Daisy broke down half a mile from the phone booth, and that's not very near Marigold Bottom. You can check for yourself."

"How did you get her to move in the end?" asked Crook curiously.

"You could say it was the power of prayer. Anyway, I knew I couldn't risk not turning up at the market in time. Old man Moss is my prospective father-in-law, as if you didn't know, and of all the tightwads . . ."

"You miss my market and you can have your cards? Well, that's the business world for you."

"Mind you, if it wasn't for Sally, I'd have asked for my cards weeks ago. Still, it's only till October. You didn't mention your witness's name," he added.

"I didn't, did I?" Crook agreed.

"What's he been telling you? That he saw me coming out of the wood with my hands stained with gore?"

"Well, of course he didn't. I told you he's a doctor, he'd know better than most that if you suffocate a girl you don't leave her lying in a pool of blood. He doesn't even say he saw you, just that he saw the lorry."

"Why didn't he go to the police right away, then?"

"Same reason as you, I suppose. Didn't think he had anything definite to tell them, and they'd want to know what he was doing in the lane, and mightn't fancy his story about trying to get a breather. Those medicos have to be like the detergents you read about, whiter than white, though what that is when it's at home don't ask me."

"Could be he fancied a bit of feminine company," suggested Terry shrewishly.

"He could say the same about you."

"I tell you I never set eyes on any sheilah. Anyway, Sally 'ud mark me for life if she thought I was carrying on with someone else, tiger cats wouldn't be in it . . ."

"Talk about standing in jeopardy every hour," Crook murmured. "St. Paul," he added in explanatory tones.

"He's not the only one," Terry observed, and his tone was a warning one. "You want to be careful—you and your pal—the way you go spreading the dirt. I don't have to go around picking up stray birds, I've got a girl of my own. And anyway, I never did care for the skinny type." He thought again of Sally, as delightfully rounded as a plump young robin, the right height, the right shape—he sent Crook a glance that might have frozen the phoenix, only Crook had become inured to those glances over the years. You keep out of my backyard, was what they meant, but for all his figure no one could teach Crook anything about climbing in by the back door or putting an eye as round and brown as a bull's-eye at an appropriate keyhole.

"Well, I daresay we'll be meeting again in court," said Crook.

"You won't see me in any bleeding court," Terry promised him.

"Never heard of a subpoena? I've got to get all the help I can for my client."

"If you're looking to me, you're looking in the wrong direction. And while you're about it you can tell your pal that if he or anyone else tries to muck things up between Sally and me he's going to wish he'd never been born, and quite soon he'll forget he ever was born. And I mean that," he wound up impressively.

"I believe you," said Crook. He did, too. This young chap and Frankie had something in common, both being defiant, young and headstrong, but if it came to a choice of meeting one or the other in the lane on a dark night, Crook knew which way his chips would fall. "Still, why should you care? You've only got to produce one of the chaps you telephoned, one of the ones who couldn't oblige you that night . . ."

Terry stared. "You gone loco? I don't have to explain to anyone, I'm not in the picture at all. I don't know who the girl had come to meet or if she'd come to meet anyone, because I didn't see her, I don't know who killed her, or who stowed her away under the bushes. I can only tell you who it wasn't and that was me. You can sick all the police of the county on to me and I can't tell them anything different. And I never saw this pal of yours, and it seems to me pretty rum he should happen to be in the lane that particular night. I suppose he couldn't have got his dates mixed."

"There'd be the death certificate," said Crook solemnly. "For the mother he didn't save, I mean. No, he's got his date all right. Funny thing is you didn't notice him going past you. But of course you were probably trying to contact all these garages. Happen to mention to Joe about Daisy breaking down?"

"By the time I'd got her going, and she went like an old lady on one leg, Joe had packed up and gone, and you can make what you like of that. If you take my tip you'll start trying to find out where your precious Frankie Piper was that night, and if he wasn't in the lane I'll eat my hat."

"So it's lucky for you you don't wear one," said Crook.

But after Terry had flung out, disregarding Crook's suggestion of a refill, the London lawyer sat pretty glumly until the barman, thinking he knew the source of his trouble, came up with a fresh tankard.

"Now why didn't you approach the police?" he asked of the invisible Terry Lamb as he downed the contents. "You had your own reasons for not wanting your presence in the lane that night to be public property." The other drivers probably knew he used the lane most nights, but they weren't likely to grass. Mind your own business would be their motto. Was it Moss he feared? Or Sally? And what had happened when Terry saw the girl? Because, that he had seen her, Crook had no doubt at all.

"Union is strength," Crook decided a little later. "I doubt whether Terry Lamb is the only one of us who stands in jeopardy." That at least was true. He got back into the Superb and drove off to call on Dr. Gray.

Dr. Gray's house was one of a tall sedate terrace of discolored brick, and both inside and out it had that cheerless neatness so often associated with the dwellings of those who acknowledge no family ties. A woman opened the door who perfectly matched her surroundings, and said at once, "If you've come to see the doctor he's not at home. There's a note of his surgery hours on the door."

"Oh, I wouldn't want to trespass on those," said Crook sunnily. The woman reminded him of someone, the Medusa perhaps, minus that worthy's beauty that turned all her lovers into stone. He could almost hear the snakes hissing in her hair. "Is he likely to be long—before he gets back, I mean?"

"Have you an appointment?" the woman wanted to know.

"If I had an appointment I suppose I'd have found him at home. But he does know me and I promised to keep in touch. Mutual advantage," he added with another of his alligator grins. "How about me coming in to wait?"

"I'm afraid there would be no use. I've no notion when he'll be back, and some days he telephones that he won't be back to lunch at all. If this is a professional visit . . ."

"Well, professional for me but not for him," said Crook as though that explained everything. He looked over his bony shoulder into the dark tidy uninspired hall. "Nice place you've got here," he offered.

She didn't trouble to answer that as inexorably the door started to close.

"I mean," Crook persisted, "you wouldn't like to lose it. Jobs like this don't grow on trees, I daresay."

"I can't imagine what you are talking about," said the woman icily. "I've been with Dr. Gray for more than seven years . . ."

"And I bet they were the best seven years of your life," agreed Crook in enthusiastic tones. "Still, if anything were to happen to the good doctor, if he were to vanish, say, the job would go with him, wouldn't it, and you'd be left lamenting?"

The housekeeper didn't precisely open the door to welcome him in, but at least the crack didn't narrow.

"If this is a publicity trick," she began, and then a fresh thought struck her. "You're not the police?"

"I'd have to declare an interest if I were, wouldn't I? Anyway, is he expecting them?"

"Not so far as I know, though I daresay from time to time they ask for his assistance, but that's true of all of us."

He gave her another of his big unrewarded smiles. "Still, I'm making a nice change, because I've come to offer assistance and not ask for it."

"If you leave your name I'll see he gets the message," said the woman, and inexorably the door began to close once more. But this time Crook didn't care, because his quick ear had caught the sound of a car slowing down by the gate, and when he turned, there was Dr. Gray getting out and not, to tell truth, looking a whit more pleased at the sight of his visitor than his housekeeper had done.

"Stars in their courses!" ejaculated Crook piously.

The doctor slammed the door of the little black saloon and came striding up the path. "You don't waste much time," he remarked.

"Always keep your partner informed of developments, that's a sovereign rule," Crook explained. "That's how me and Bill—still, you don't want to hear about him. I was just asking could I wait . . ."

"You'd better come in," said Gray briefly. "Any messages, Mrs. Thrupp?"

"I've put them on your table, Doctor. And you have an appointment at twelve-fifteen."

"I'll be gone before then," Crook promised obligingly.

"What's new?" the doctor inquired when they were in what was presumably the doctor's consulting room.

"Regard me as the voice of one crying in the wilderness," Crook offered. "I've trailed your chap in the lorry. He don't deny that he was there that night, he don't deny that he left the lorry unattended—a bust-up, he says—while he went along to try and contact a garage, but he says it wasn't by Marigold Bottom but quite a piece along the road."

"Perhaps it was when the lorry broke down," the doctor agreed. "I'm only telling you that when I saw it, it was standing quite near the Bottom. I never saw the chap, and if he was phoning—I suppose that's what you mean—from the box along the road you'd have expected me to see him."

"Not if he was having fun and games with the girl in the wood, I wouldn't," retorted Crook. "And by the time he came out you'd be gone."

"Yes. That's true. I suppose he says he didn't see the girl?"

"He says he didn't go to the police because he couldn't tell them anything that would be any use—he didn't see your car and he didn't see you; he didn't see anyone but a chap on a motorbike who went past at the speed of light."

"Did he explain why he didn't go to the police?"

"Didn't want the limelight, he's got a young lady of his own who's the possessive type and he don't want to spend his married life going round with a guide dog for the blind. That's what he says. The fact is," continued Crook thoughtfully, "I rather fancy he did see that girl, which don't, of course, mean he killed her."

"What makes you say that?"

"He said he don't fancy the skinny type, and what was her mum thinking about letting a kid like that go around on her own? Well, she was eighteen. Young women of eighteen are wives and mums themselves, only it's a fact she did look a lot younger, according to all accounts, only how did he know? And then there's the fact that the lorry was stashed where you saw it, and that's quite a piece from the phone box."

"I suppose he's got an alibi for the rest of the evening," Gray suggested.

"He got his load to the market just in time, but he wasn't seen by anyone."

"But the lorry . . ."

"According to him he finally got her working on his owney-oh. Now, that's the kind of story the police like to tear apart, only if he can't prove where he was, no more can they. Oh, and he says it's not surprising no one saw her if she was walking on the far side of the hedge, only the state of her shoes don't seem to bear out that notion."

"That's true, of course," the doctor allowed. "The hedges there are pretty tall and she was a small-made girl. Are you reporting any of this to the police?"

Crook looked surprised. "I haven't got anything to tell them yet, have I? You and me may work on hunches but not the slops."

"I suppose he couldn't have been meeting the girl . . ."

"Oh, be your age," counseled Crook rudely. "Nobody, not even the girl herself, knew she was going to be in the lane that night. Too bad he can't get anyone to alibi his story about ringing the garages, but—can you believe it?—everyone was having a Bank Holiday that night. And nobody came along the lane . . ."

"It was pretty deserted," the doctor admitted. "I don't recall seeing anyone else, and if anyone saw me they didn't report it."

"Probably wouldn't have noticed you, but a dirty great lorry jamming the road, that's another pair of dancing pumps. The fact is, the lorries don't use that road any more, and young Lamb, that's the name, Terry Lamb, ain't supposed to either. Only he's not the type who likes being told what he may do. And seeing his boss is also his prospective father-in-law and is just looking for an excuse to bust up the engagement, and also," he continued like a member of Parliament winding up a successful peroration, "see-ing that old man Moss is very warm and young Terry's the type whose pockets always have holes in them, you do see why he thinks discretion is the better part of valor. So that," he wound up, "is why I'm here. Just to give you the wigwag."

"What on earth does that mean?"

"Just keep your eye on your driving mirror and remember, like I told him, that chaps wearing our shoes stand in jeopardy every hour. It's worth bearing in mind that when a car comes into collision with a lorry it isn't usually the lorry or its driver who pays the penalty."

The doctor looked shocked. "You're not suggesting this chap might try and run me down?"

"He'd sleep a lot quieter of nights if you were out of the way. Oh, I know you haven't told the police anything yet, but you could."

"So could you," retorted the doctor tartly.

Crook shook his big ginger head. "What the soldier heard ain't evidence. I've only got your story, and though it ain't always true that dead men tell no tales, at all events they can't pop up in witness boxes. Now—who else have you told?"

"No one," said Gray. "I didn't want to involve this fellow— what did you say his name was?—Lamb unless it became necessary. Then the police picked up Piper and there was no reason to suppose they hadn't adequate grounds . . . then you appeared and, as I say, I felt I must speak to someone, and frankly, from my point of view you're a better bet than the police."

"Well, then," said Crook in reasonable tones, "you do see it would be to X's advantage if you were somewhere where you couldn't give evidence."

"Did you tell this chap who I was?" asked Gray abruptly.

"No. Why should I? Do you suppose I want to be accessory before the act? Mind you, he's no fool, he could find out, I suppose. I don't know what he drives when he isn't at the wheel of his lorry, though I suppose it shouldn't be impossible to find out. Only in my experience fellows who're out to make trouble often borrow someone else's car."

"I doubt whether our paths are likely to cross," observed the doctor rather stiffly.

"That 'ud depend on Terry, wouldn't it? He's a night driver, remember, which gives him a lot of daylight to play around in."

"I can't make any definite accusation," Gray pointed out. "This chap must have the sense to realize that. I didn't see anyone, I couldn't even swear the lorry wasn't driven by a woman—they seem to be around everywhere these days—and—isn't this a bit odd?—I didn't hear anything."

"That was the idea," said Crook politely. "Why he got his hand over her mouth—I suppose she was going to give the alarm to anything or anyone within earshot—could be he heard your car, though according to the medical evidence there was no attempt at criminal assault. Anyway, hearing, unless you went to investigate, wouldn't help a lot. I understand Alcock's going to prosecute; he's not exactly my favorite man but he knows his onions. You wouldn't be ten minutes in the witness box before you'd be wondering if you'd really been in the lane that night at all, let alone heard any sounds from behind the hedge. No, I'm here as the still small voice—warning, you know."

"So you said," the doctor agreed. "Am I intended to take you seriously?"

"Up to you," said Crook. "But—someone killed that girl and it wasn't my client."

"You think it was young Lamb?"

Crook widened his eyes. "I don't know, do I? But someone did. And if you recall, I didn't say just look in your driving mirror for Terry, just look in it for anyone who might seem to be taking more interest than usual in your movements. Y'see, now you've come to me the heat's on. So long as you kept your trap shut you were in the clear. You didn't go to the police, you didn't talk to the press. X might argue, well, you had your own reasons for wanting to stay out of the limelight. Now you've come to me."

"And he'll know that?"

"He'll find out, if he doesn't. The successful killers are the ones who don't bother. I mean, they knock off their enemy or whatever and then sit back and wait. But the others, they want to play safe; when they come round the corner and find instead of an empty road a lion in the way, they don't walk past the lion, they pull out their little popgun or their bit of poisoned steak. If ever you're tempted to commit a murder, you take the word of the man who knows: let the other side do the work, and half the time at least you'll find they do it wrong—same like they have here."

"Does he strike you as the killer type—Lamb, I mean?" the doctor demanded.

"There's no special type, except the loonies who kill for fun," Crook explained. "You should know that as well as me. We're all potential killers." He thought of the great war, a world away now, when he'd lied himself into the army at the age of seventeen, and had been swallowed up in an enormous pool of anonymity. He'd often thought how pleasant it 'ud be to black someone's eye or push him into the gutter, but he'd never have carried a knife or boasted of brass knuckles. All the same, he'd killed when the day's work seemed to demand it. And this chap, too, a doctor, he must have some raw memories; even if he hadn't willed death he must have sat at bedsides and watched the approach and known his own helplessness.

If I'm not careful, thought Crook, coming abruptly to his senses, I'll end up a lady novelist.

"It's a matter of self-defense as often as not," he explained. "You or him. If he'd come clean about the girl, any good counsel would have got him a verdict of manslaughter, she wasn't the kind that got men into a frenzy. And Terry can take his pick, take my word for that. Probably been rolling 'em all like rabbits since he was sixteen. That chap could whistle a hippopotamus out of its pond in a heat wave. Frankie couldn't have put one over on old Mrs. Nick, not from what I've heard of her, but Terry might persuade her into believing he was a messenger from on high."

"You like your pictures very fancy," the doctor said.

"Well, I do, and that's a fact," Crook acknowledged. "Only I didn't make the picture, you know. If I had I expect I'd have made it different. But I'm like those chaps in the Old Testament who had to make their bricks with the straw they had, and if there wasn't any straw lying around they had to go out and find it."

"And that's what you're doing now?"

"It's the only way," said Crook. "Of course, you could go to the police with the story you told me. The press 'ud eat it, and once the slops knew . . ."

"They might think it a bit odd that I hadn't approached them before," said the doctor. "They might think it very convenient that I should suddenly remember seeing the lorry minus its driver. And whatever construction they put on the story, it 'ud ruin my future. I'm not a career man, Mr. Crook, I told you, didn't I? And I don't play cards. If I did I might have played this hand better."

"Might be worth considering all the same," Crook told him.

"For whose sake?" inquired Gray shrewdly. "Mine? Or your client's?"

"Well, all of us," Crook conceded.

But he was pretty sure the doctor wouldn't take his hint, and in a way you couldn't blame him. He'd got himself into a nasty fix, and it isn't enough for innocence to exist, it's got to be shown to exist.

"Time's running out," he added, suddenly opening the door and nearly falling over Mrs. Thrupp, who was in the hall for some reason. It seemed a rum time to be dusting the immaculate furniture, but that was no business of his. He got back into the Superb and drove away.

And from his place of concealment Murder watched him go.

XI

"THIS IS THE TIME to keep your peepers open," Crook had told the doctor. "This is when X is likely to strike, so keep your eyes on your driving mirror."

It was like going around in a circle—Terry Lamb warning him, Crook passing on the warning to the doctor and getting it passed back. But though he kept a fairly stiff lookout on his return journey he couldn't see anyone definitely on the trail. He didn't know, of course, what vehicle a pursuer might be using, but it's not easy to engineer a street accident in a busy thoroughfare without a lot of uncomfortable questions being asked. He would have told you he wasn't a superstitious man, but he did get a slight shock when he passed a trail of sandwichmen dragging their steps in the gutter and carrying boards that proclaimed: The Day of the Lord Is at Hand. And in point of fact the tide had turned, and it wasn't just a case of the water seeping back gently over the sand, but something more in the nature of a tidal wave.

He stopped at the Golden Goose for a pint and a snack, and when he came into his lodgings he was made aware that the war was definitely on. Mrs. Fred came to meet him.

"There's been a call for you, Mr. Crook," she said. "On the phone. You just missed it."

"Stopped off at the Goose," Crook explained. "Who was it? Or didn't he leave a name?"

"It was a funny sort of call," Mrs. Fred allowed. "From one of these coin boxes, so it couldn't be your friend from London."

Crook and Bill kept up a two-way traffic on the phone that made her shudder to think what the account would look like when it came in.

"No name?" suggested Crook, raising his big red brows.

143

"Well, no. When I said you weren't back he just rung off."

"Not even a message. Well, if it's important he'll come through again. Seeing he didn't leave his moniker, he can't expect me to call him."

It went to show, though, that Murder was beginning to get ants in his pants, and from Crook's viewpoint the sooner they cleared up the affair and let him go back to his beloved London the better. What he mainly had to be concerned about, in addition to getting Frankie Piper off the hook, of course, was to get there in one piece. He added considerably to his telephone bill before he went back to his room and settled down to dealing with stuff that his partner had forwarded, and it wasn't till fairly late that afternoon that he got the next call. But there was no mystery about this one. The chap at the other end of the line was Dr. Gray and he sounded not so much apprehensive as huffed.

"Ring me earlier?" Crook inquired, and the doctor said no, why should he, he'd only just had this call himself.

"No name?" said Crook, and Gray asked sarcastically, "How did you guess?"

"What was the message?" inquired Crook, unperturbed. "Tell you to go jump in the river?"

"Well, not precisely, but it was a threat all the same."

"Anonymous calls generally are. If they weren't they wouldn't be anonymous."

"He said the police might be interested to know where I was the night that girl was killed. So clearly he knows who I am."

"That does seem to follow," Crook acknowledged. "Wonder if Terry Lamb's been approached. Well, take care of yourself. I'd say zero hour is near."

"I suppose it's always easy to be philosophical at someone else's expense," the doctor said. "I suppose if I'd been in my right mind I'd have gone to the police at the start . . ."

"Only you didn't want your name mixed up with a sordid case like this," Crook finished for him. "It's always a sordid case where a young girl's concerned. And you couldn't know which way the cat was going to jump." He thought for a moment, then added, "By the way, how was it made, the call, I mean? Home number or a call box?"

"Now you come to mention it, I believe it was a call box. I hadn't thought about it . . ."

"Well, it just shows he knows his onions," Crook consoled him. "If you or me were making threatening calls we'd use a call box, too. Can't be traced, see. And much safer than anonymous letters, which are a trap and a delusion if anything ever was."

"I didn't recognize the voice," the doctor volunteered.

Crook actually laughed. "I don't suppose I'd have recognized the voice that called me. That 'ud be part of the setup."

He tried the telephone number of the house where Terry had his digs and found the driver was in.

"Didn't try and get me on the blower a bit earlier in the day, I suppose?" Crook said, and Terry asked, "What gave you that idea?"

"Someone rang when I was out and I'm trying to track the call. Incidentally, I suppose no nameless chap's been trying to contact you?"

"Why should they?" Terry demanded.

"Fair do's," explained Crook. "The doctor and me have both had a shot across the bows. But perhaps X don't think you could be dangerous. I mean, you don't know anything, do you?"

"I told you," Terry began.

"So you did. Only sometimes, when chaps have a bit of time to think, they recall things they'd forgotten earlier."

"Not in this case," Terry assured him, but when he had hung up he did a spell of thinking, which was fairly unusual for him.

What's he driving at? he wondered. He's got nothing on me, nothing. There are no witnesses . . . None who could go into the box, he meant, and though it's not always true that dead men (and women) tell no tales, they can't tell them on oath, and that's what matters. I'm in the clear, he assured himself. He didn't think about Frankie Piper. The chap was a nutter anyway, going into the old woman's house and leaving a trail of evidence against him, and expecting the police to believe his story. Anyway, he had Crook to look after him, and the age of chivalry has been dead for a long time. No one hangs around any more waiting for someone else to go out of the door first, and if there's a queue a wise man's place is at the head of it, no matter how he gets there.

As soon as he'd hung up, Crook rang the doctor's number. "Nothing from Terry Lamb," he said. "But it wouldn't do you any harm not to open any doors tonight, or tell your housekeeper to look out of the window before she does, and remember—the uniform don't necessarily make the man."

"Mrs. Thrupp isn't here tonight," the doctor said. "She doesn't sleep in, goes off after she's given me my dinner. But thanks for the warning."

"And watch out for any sick calls," Crook added.

"You do the same," the doctor told him.

"All of us playing puss-in-the-corner," Crook murmured. "But if puss never comes out of his corner . . ."

"It's all one big joke to you, isn't it?" the doctor exploded. But Crook, suddenly grave, said murder was never a joke, especially not to the chap on the mortuary slab.

He might sound frivolous enough on the blower, but back in his room he scowled. He didn't like the situation, he didn't like it one little bit. He was still brooding when Mrs. Fred looked in to say she was going out for half an hour to see her neighbor, Mrs. Eason, so if Mr. Crook's call hadn't come through . . . She paused inquiringly. Crook said no, it hadn't, most likely it wouldn't, but he'd keep his ear open. He grinned as he spoke, but without his normal buoyancy. There had been corpses enough in this case, and if he wasn't careful there might well be another, and it was up to him, Mr. Conjurer Crook, to see that didn't happen.

"I've got a lovely bit of liver for your supper," Mrs. Fred said. "Fred fancies a bit of liver." But Crook's discomfort seemed to have communicated itself to her. "You all right, Mr. Crook?"

"As of now," Crook agreed, but without the merry quip she'd come to look for. "Tomorrow now, that's another story."

"Were you expecting something tomorrow, then?"

Crook dragged up another rusty quote from his rag bag of a memory. "Tomorrow I may be myself with someone or other's thousand years," he told her.

Mrs. Fred shook her head. These southerners. It was a pity they didn't teach them to talk ordinary Queen's English. What on earth had a thousand years to do with today? Even Mr. Crook 'ud be dead and buried and forgotten long before then. All the same, she was worried.

"Why don't you talk to Mr. Doyle about it?" she suggested. "He'll be at the Goose tonight, and he's got a lot of sense, has Joseph. Living in the country like, he knows how folks' minds work."

Mrs. Fred had been gone for some time when he heard the shot. At first he thought he must be mistaken, it was a bursting tire. It was a thing that often happened in a city, and he went to the little balcony opening off his room to look out. But there didn't seem to be any vehicle in distress; in fact, there didn't seem to be any vehicle at all. This was a quiet back street, and everyone was at the local or the bingo or tucking in to a good north country high tea. The silence irked him, he liked to feel himself part of the whirling colored pattern of city life. Silence wasn't natural, not once the world was created, and he'd never hankered for a time before the Holy Spirit brooded over chaos. Life wasn't intended for tranquillity, there'd be plenty of that in the grave, and he suspected the surface calm of country life. If danger was abroad he preferred it to be in the open. In the country too much went on underground.

Under the window from the shades of the shrubbery someone gave a groan. Crook leaned further out. If chaps were going to take their own lives they might do it in a decent privacy. The second shot coincided with a sudden backward move on his part, as the hunch that had preserved him so often during his passage through the valley of affliction (not his phrase but a telling one for all that) stabbed him as sharply as a hatpin, so that the bullet intended for his heart went astray and caught him in the shoulder and dropped him like an ox. And like a fallen ox he lay, with the blood seeping out of him, and no more sense in his noodle than a ruddy great turnip.

The man in the shadows stood as still as the bushes that concealed him, waiting for someone to give the alarm, but nothing happened. Behind closed windows wirelesses played, people concentrated on the box, glasses clinked. Mrs. Fred had bustled off,

Fred was at the Goose. So when the coast remained clear, the watcher crept out of his hiding place and went away.

At the Golden Goose they wondered what was detaining Mr. Crook.

"Southerner or no, you're going to miss that man, Fred," said P. C. Doyle.

"Funny thing." Fred nodded solemnly. "Though you could say he was—what's that word?—a cosmopolitan. Makes himself at home anywhere. One thing, he has added a bit of life to the place."

"All through being concerned with death," agreed Doyle, who could usually be relied upon to say the unexpected thing. "It's to be hoped he'll spare a bit of thought for himself, though. Stands to reason, a man like that will have enemies."

At Mrs. Eason's they were also discussing Crook, though from a somewhat different angle.

"If it was me I wouldn't be able to sleep of nights, not with that man in the house," said Mrs. Eason firmly. "You mark my words, Beattie, something will come of this, it's not natural, it's not as if he was a policeman." Meaning that the uniform of the police constitutes a certain protection. "All very well for him to take his life in his hands, he should think of you and Fred."

"Makes a change," said Mrs. Fred sturdily. "It's not always a good thing to get into a rut."

And then she changed the subject, asking about Mrs. Eason's daughter-in-law, and Mrs. Eason perked up and said would you believe it, she'd got another bun in the oven, and there was such a thing as moderation. It wasn't as if they hadn't got five kids already. One way and another the time slipped past and Mrs. Fred was shocked to see she was going to have her work cut out to get Fred's liver cooked when he came in panting for it. He was a good chap as husbands go, but he didn't like being kept waiting for his food, and you couldn't blame him. Men were all the same. He came in just as she was putting the last slice of liver onto the big blue dish she'd bought at the Christmas jumble.

"Mr. Crook not around?" he asked.

"Why, didn't he come to the Goose? P'raps he got that call he was waiting for, after all."

"Not like Mr. Crook to wait for anyone. Mr. Doyle had his pint set up, too."

"I daresay that didn't go to waste," observed Mrs. Fred. But she was looking less satisfied now.

"What is it, Mother?" He only called her Mother when he was a bit bothered about something himself.

"He didn't look himself when I went up to tell him I was going to pop round and see Alice. And there was this call. I didn't like the sound of it. Just go up and make sure he's all right, Fred. He mightn't have heard us come in."

"He'll have heard all right," prophesied Fred. "There's one will hear from the wrong side of a coffin lid."

But he went up all the same, tapped on the door, got no reply, opened it and walked in to find the French window flapping in the breeze. This was unusual; Crook wasn't one of your open-air types, a good healthy fug was his choice.

He's never fallen over the balcony, thought Fred in a moment of rare panic, which increased when a moment later he almost fell over Crook's prostrate body, then went tearing to the door to tell Beattie to call the doctor and then come upstairs.

"Remember something he said not a day or two back," he reminded her while they waited for Dr. Morton. "Too bad I didn't bring my crystal ball with me, save us a lot of trouble. Well, you must have had yours tonight, a pity you didn't see more clearly what was going to happen."

It was odd, seeing what a clumping four-square sort of chap Mr. Crook was, the fuss that was made over his "dilemma," a pressman's word that. It wasn't just the local rags who sent their representatives to get a story, the nationals were represented, too. There was even a message about him on the B.B.C. Dr. Gray heard this when he put the news on that night. Still unconscious, they reported, condition serious, doctor wouldn't commit himself. No clue to the attacker to date, or if there was they weren't telling. It was common knowledge he was in the district on Frankie Piper's account, but since he generally kept his own counsel it began to seem as though no one would be able to identify his attacker. The pressboys hung around, drinking the good ale at the Golden Goose and generally pestering everyone. Mrs. Fred got her picture in the paper, and a proper caricature it was. Not that they got anywhere. It was like trying to bust open a safe when you didn't know the combination, as one remarked to another. Dr. Gray wondered about ringing up the hospital and asking for news, but since his name hadn't so far been associated with the affair (and nothing I can tell the police will help them, he argued, meaning that all they wanted to know was the name of the chap who'd fired the shot) he emulated the Tar Baby, who laid low and said nuffin.

When Crook came around, about twenty-four hours after the attack, the first face he saw was a stranger's. The room was unfamiliar, too. They'd given him a private room at the hospital; they couldn't have police and pressmen upsetting their nice quiet ward. Anyway, seeing he was giving them more excitement than they'd had for a month of Sundays, they reckoned he deserved something.

Crook's eyes came back from the plain, uninspiring walls to his companion's face. "Who are you?" he inquired baldly.

"I'll ask the questions" was the reply, and Crook gave a great chuckle that died out somewhat ruefully.

"Don't tell me I'm in the nick?" he exploded. "I didn't know they did you so well."

"You're in hospital, of course, and there's a queue of chaps all waiting to talk to you, headed by the police."

"P. C. Doyle," asked Crook eagerly. "No, of course not. It'll be that inspector. Before he comes, put me in the picture. How did I get here?"

"By ambulance. How do you suppose? And you're right about it being Inspector Mount. And I may tell you he's not pleased with the situation, he's not pleased at all."

"Difficult chap to satisfy," murmured Crook. "I'd have thought he'd be delighted. Or does he feel he's wasted his money on a premature wreath?"

"He's going to want a pretty detailed explanation of how you landed yourself here."

"You've just told me. In an ambulance. What was I doing there?"

"If you don't know, no one does. I think I'll tell that police wallah you're not fit for questioning yet, your mind's a blank . . ."

"Did I say that?" asked Crook. "Must have been talking in my sleep."

"Don't strain yourself," urged the doctor. "Naturally, they'll want your story, how you came to be shot . . ."

Crook winced. "I'm getting past it," he confessed frankly, and he clearly wasn't himself or he'd never have made such an admission. "That's the oldest trick in the book and I fell for it like a two-year-old. Where was I?"

"When they found you? On the balcony. Funny thing, I should never have suspected you of being a nature lover."

"I feel about nature like people who don't like dogs feel about dogs—very nice for other people if they're kept in the right place. No, of course I wasn't admiring nature, but there was this shot . . ." He paused. "No, there were two shots. The first one was to lure me out, and that's just what it did. There I stood, a bloody great target . . ."

"Lucky for you he wasn't a first-class shot," commented the doctor smoothly.

"It could be I moved," Crook offered.

"Whatever you did was pretty uncooperative. I don't think you were meant to be able to pool your information with the police. Still, a miss is as good as a mile, and what's a bullet a few inches away from your heart to a chap with your reputation?"

Crook's thoughts were proceeding along his own particular lines. "If this story gets around London, I may as well hang up my *Retired* card and apply for my pension," he observed grimly.

"Talking of London," said the doctor, "there's a character here, name of Parsons, lurking on the other side of the door."

"Don't tell me Bill's losing his grip too," marveled Crook. "This time last year he'd have battered the door down if he found it locked."

The doctor sighed. "You must like a rough house, we take things more easily here. No, he slept in the hospital last night, like a dog outside master's door. I'd be sorry for anyone who gets in his path. No wonder the Metropolitan police usually give the pair of you best."

"Don't know what he thinks he can do here," complained Crook. "He should be looking after our interests at the other end. Still, you have to admit X is a trier—the girl, old Mrs. Nick, now me, and we can't be certain it'll stop there."

"In his shoes I'd be discouraged by now," said the doctor.

"He can't afford to be discouraged; that's the worst of starting a game like this, you can't opt out when it suits you. There's method in his madness, you know. I mean, he's not just a killer running amok with a knife for the fun of it."

"He should have stopped at the girl," said the doctor simply. "He could have got away with manslaughter if he'd had a counsel worth his salt. In his shoes I'd have urged status lymphaticus, a thyroid condition in which any sort of shock can prove fatal. He'll find it a lot more difficult to talk himself out of the charge concerning the old woman. She may have had a mortal disease, but it wasn't shock that killed her, and who was he to put a period to her days?"

"Everyone spoke as if she was immortal," Crook protested.

"I don't know about being immortal," said Morton grimly. "You'd have to ask the chaplain about that. But she had Howard's disease, and I daresay she knew it. Didn't I hear she was a doctor's daughter and his unofficial assistant? She may never have taken any training but early knowledge sticks. No, she very likely knew, but she doesn't sound the sort to chat about it."

"It would add up," reflected Crook. "Her reluctance to go to the niece. The husband's a doctor; I daresay he'd have realized what was wrong."

"He'd have realized all right. It's a fairly uncommon disease and it only attacks the old, and so far it's incurable. I don't say we shall never know how to treat it, but to date . . ." He spread his hands. "You could argue he'd done her a favor, she wouldn't have gone out so easy if she'd finished her course the way nature intended. Still, you can't expect the law to take that point of view. And of course," he wound up frankly, "he must have been crazy to take that pot shot at you. What was the idea anyhow?"

"Stop me opening my big mouth. So long as I was around he

was about as safe as Little Black Sambo when the crocodiles came calling."

"The police have identified the bullet," the doctor said.

"And I daresay there aren't more than about five million like it knocking around the country," Crook agreed. "But I'll promise you this—when you've nailed your chap and start going through his effects, the one thing you won't find is a gun license. Come to that," he added, "the odds are you won't find a gun either."

A step sounded in the passage, accompanied by a wave of half-articulate protest. The door was pushed open and a saturnine face appeared in the entry.

"Hi, Bill," said Crook.

"Mr. Parsons," said the sister, who looked about as capable of deflecting the tall thin figure from its purpose as a kitten trying to shut the door on a gorilla, "you've been told you can't come into a patient's room except during visiting hours. Mr. Crook has been on the danger list, and in any case the police have priority."

"That's what they've been thinking for the past thirty years," said Bill. "You'd expect them to have developed a bit of know-how by now."

"A police officer has been waiting for some hours." Sister looked at Dr. Morton. "Is the patient able to answer questions?"

"Do him good," said Crook heartlessly. "As for being on the danger list, danger list for whom?"

"Doctor," the sister began, and Morton said, "You'd better ask him. 'Fore God I am no coward, but I'm not taking any chances of this one slipping through my fingers. They'd be playing the Dead March in Saul for me within the week if that happened."

"Before you bring anyone in," suggested Crook, "no harm in remembering the uniform don't make the man."

Sister looked as if she could have thrust a skewer through his black complacent heart. This—this thing from the zoo—presuming to advise her! She began to feel some sympathy for the man who had held the gun. "They may do things differently in London," she said coldly, "but here we know our policemen."

"Famous last words," murmured Crook.

"How about it, Mr. Crook?" the doctor said.

"I have a very funny feeling," Crook told him. "I don't think

I'm ready to answer questions yet."

"Tell him to hang on awhile longer," said the doctor.

Sister looked outraged. "If Mr. Crook's able to see Mr. Parsons . . ."

"It's not that I ain't up to seeing him," Crook explained, "it's just that I don't know what I can tell him." He turned to the doctor. "Do you ever get the feeling, when you're looking inside a chaps stomach, say—do you find yourself murmuring, 'I wish I could be sure what this was.' "

"More likely to wish I didn't know," the doctor returned. "What's happened? He's beginning to wander," he added to Sister.

"It's something I've just learned," said Crook. "Only I'm not sure—it's like a will-o-the-wisp . . ." He flapped a huge mutton-like fist. "Or when you strike a light and it goes out before you can see what you lit it for."

"Feverish!" was Sister's grim comment. "I knew how it would be."

"Do you blame him?" asked the doctor. "Most men in his circumstances 'ud be dead by now."

"Now, don't go putting ideas into Sister's noodle," Crook besought him. "And, Sister, tell that rozzer to stay on the alert, because any minute now the dawn may break, and when it does the balloon 'ull go up so fast . . ."

"Mr. Parsons," Sister began as the doctor came to his feet.

"Oh, let him stay," said Morton easily. It was obvious Bill intended to stay anyhow. "No harm to humor the patient. We let kids have their mothers nowadays, so why not the friend that sticketh closer than a brother? You might be glad afterward, you never know. A bodyguard in circumstances like these never comes amiss."

Sister drew herself erect. "Surely, Doctor, you don't suppose . . ."

"Never heard of taking two bites at a cherry? If X couldn't afford to let Mr. Crook go on breathing before, he's got twice as much reason to want to shut him up now. And seeing how short-handed you are, how you manage what you do defeats me—" Gently he edged her out of the room.

XII

WHEN THE DOCTOR and the sister had retired, Bill wandered over to the window. Not that there was much to see. He waited for Crook to break the silence. Crook lay back against his pillows, saying nothing. At last Bill observed, "Ann Piper rang the office when she heard the news. Very distressed."

"Any sympathy gratefully received," Crook murmured.

"Sympathy? She was kicking herself for having found a lawyer for her husband who was careless enough to get himself nearly knocked off."

"If you can't beat 'em join 'em," said Crook. "There's times I wonder if Frankie isn't better off in prison. We seem to have struck a right daft lot this time—bossy Mrs. Piper; that girl who was more than half round the bend, if the doctor can be believed; a dying old woman . . ." He stopped. "Bill, that's it."

Bill stood very stiff by the window, as if he thought a sudden movement might distract Crook's thought processes.

"A dying woman," Crook repeated. "That's it. And I had the card in my hand all this time and I didn't even know it was a trump. At this rate, I'll end up in the geriatric ward yet. Bill, has there been another violent death in the neighborhood while I've been lying here like a stuck pig, and they won't tell me because I'm in a delicate state and must be spared?"

"If there has been, the police are lying doggo about it. You're getting all the headlines *pro tem.*"

"Wheel that inspector in," said Crook, pulling himself more erect against the pillows. The room was beginning to move around him, walls bulging. "Don't you go, Bill," he added. "If the slops are entitled to have a witness to their interviews, the poor bloody B. P. should have the same privilege."

155

Bill went out and returned a minute or so later with Inspector Mount and Sister very much in charge.

"Five minutes, Inspector," she announced. "That's all the doctor will permit."

"In that case," said Crook, as the door closed, "I'll do the talking."

Mount dropped easily into a chair beside the bed. He looked as if he was enjoying himself. David might have looked like that when he saw Goliath prone at his feet.

"This is a pretty kettle of fish, Mr. Crook," he remarked.

"Depends how much you like fish. You know Bill Parsons, my alter ego." He brought out the phrase with tremendous aplomb. "First, has there been another secret murder that you're sitting on? Go on, I'm not joking."

Mount shook his head. "If so, I haven't been informed."

"Then unless you want another, pull in a chap called Terry Lamb, he drives for a greengrocer and fruiter called Moss at Ferndown. If there hasn't been another attempt it's because my attacker hoped I was a goner, and there was a chance, or so the doctor seemed to suggest. As soon as it's known that I'm still in the land of the living you can look for more pot shots."

"Any special reason for suspecting this man, Mr. Crook?" Mount inquired.

"I told you. We want to prevent another murder."

"It's always useful if we can proffer a charge," Mount pointed out. "I don't say he isn't the one who took a pot shot at you, but have you any proof?"

Crook stared. "Well, of course I haven't any proof. Do make those walls stay still," he added pettishly. "Curtsying and bowing. Any stick'll do to beat a dog, you don't need me to tell you that. Just pull him in. If you find I'm barking up the wrong tree, but you won't, you can always say you were taking him into protective custody. That must flatter any fellow's vanity, the police thinking him so important . . ."

His voice seemed to waver a bit. Mount turned to Bill. "Mr. Parsons, I don't know if you can explain—this is the first time I've heard Lamb's name mentioned. Of course, if Mr. Crook's been holding out on us . . ."

"Ever been in a war?" Crook inquired. "Well, did you go running to the other side and make 'em a present of your chaps' plans? Of course you didn't; and of course I've been holding out on you, but now—and this may not be a record, but it's not a thing that often happens—I find myself on the same side of the police."

He signed to Bill, who produced a brandy flask as though it were the most natural thing in the world and poured Crook a shot. "I'll put the inspector in the picture while you get your breath back," he offered.

"Trust you to come up with something no one else would think of" was Mount's grim comment when Bill finished talking. He reflected that he was going to look a proper Charlie if Crook's deductions were wrong, but all the same he knew he was going to fall in with Crook's suggestions. Anything else would be too risky, and already he realized that Crook would be backed by a lot of chaps whose chief aim in life, apparently, is to make trouble for the police. "If you'd come to us at the start," he began severely, and Crook gave a shadow of his normal alligator grin.

"You'd have liked that, wouldn't you? Why, you wouldn't even have been interested, you knew it all. You had your chap all gagged and bound . . ."

"Gagged is good," remarked the inspector.

"Anything else?" Bill queried. "Matron will be back any minute, and personally I'd as soon tackle a lady dragon."

"Leave it to us," said Mount. "And take care of yourself, Mr. Crook. We've had bodies enough for one case, and we don't want you in the undertaker's parlor, not in our part of the world anyway. We've got enough of a traffic problem as it is." He actually smiled. It was amazing what it did to his face.

"Don't forget about the doctor," added Crook. "Keep an eye . . ." His voice wavered away again.

"We'll watch over him like guardian angels," Mount promised. "As for you . . ."

"I don't need any guardian angels, I've got Bill."

"If anything should happen to Mr. Crook," offered Bill gently, "you'll have your extra corpse, believe me, and I shan't think much of British justice" (not that he thought a lot of it anyway, he was like Crook in that) "if a jury doesn't bring in justifiable homicide."

"London must be a lively place," the inspector observed. "Gangs of homicidal maniacs roaming the streets . . ."

But neither of his audience was paying any attention to him. Crook's main thought was that any minute the walls would come crashing down like the walls of Jericho and he couldn't be sure Bill would be able to hold them up. The inspector hurried out, had a word with Sister—"I know he's as mad as a hatter," he said, "but keep him alive long enough to get him in the witness box"— and departed at the double to give instructions for Terry Lamb to be located and brought in, even if he was on the summit of Mount Ararat.

When Terry got to the café on the night of Crook's attack he found Williams leaning on the counter talking to Joe. When he saw Terry he grinned.

"That pal of yours seems to have some funny friends," he observed.

"Which one's that?" asked Terry, giving his usual order. Play it cool and close to the chest, he thought.

"Mr. Crook. Or hadn't you heard?"

"What's he been up to?"

"It's what someone else has been up to. Someone took a pot shot at him. It was on the late news. They've got him in hospital, police all round the bed," elaborated Williams, who liked his dish with plenty of parsley around it. "Funny, he looks as though he went around in armor-plating."

"Don't know what else he expects," said Terry unsympathetically. "Pushing his nose into other people's affairs."

"It's not his nose that got injured," said Joe.

"Well, don't look at me," Terry advised him. "I never saw the chap but once. He was after anyone who might have been in the lane the night the girl got hers, but I couldn't help him and I told him so. Period."

He never hung about long, patience was a virtue he couldn't spell, but tonight his stay was even briefer than usual. The news next morning was no more informative. Crook had had a fair night but no statement was being issued. A gent would have passed out without involving Terry Lamb, thought Terry. Still, what had he to fear? There was no proof and now there never could be any. That doctor chap had held his tongue too long to come forward at this stage, probably had something of his own to hide or he'd have surfaced before this. So—"You're in the clear," he assured himself. "You're in the clear."

Which made the shock all the greater when the police came calling at his address that same night.

"Mr. Lamb?" they asked, all very social and polite. He'd opened the door himself, his landlady being out at the shops.

"That's me," he acknowledged. "What gives?"

"Can we come in?" one of the policemen said.

"Well, it's not my house," Terry pointed out. "And my landlady wouldn't like the police here, she's not used to having uniforms around."

"In that case, p'raps you'll come with us, Mr. Lamb. Easier really."

"What are you on about?" asked Terry.

"We think you might be able to help us with our inquiries."

"Which one?"

"It's about Mr. Crook. You did hear . . ."

"Him! I don't know how you think I can help . . ."

"Just a few questions. A formality," he added encouragingly. "We're contacting everyone who knows him."

"I answered a few questions for him, that's the lot, and I couldn't help him any more than I can help you."

"The inspector might like to be the judge of that."

"And if I refuse?" Terry looked dangerous.

"You know your rights," said the policeman. "But why should you?"

"I've got a job, mate," Terry pointed out. "I'm a night driver. I can't go arsing about at police stations, Mr. Moss wouldn't like it."

"Mr. Moss 'ull know it's every citizen's job to assist the police when a crime's been committed."

A few people stopped in the street to enjoy the spectacle of some other chap being interrogated by the boys in blue.

"You'd best come in," said Terry ungraciously. "Only I warn you, you're wasting your time."

"We don't call the process of elimination a waste of time. Every name we can strike off the list narrows the field, see."

"You're joking, of course," said Terry. "If this inspector of yours thinks I can tell him anything about Crook— I only saw him the once, someone must have told him I use the lane at night, and he wondered could I help. That's all."

"Just for the record," said one of the officers, "could you tell us where you were the night he was shot?" And hastily he added a caution.

"More process of elimination?" Terry inquired. "You want your head examined; I don't know anything about him being shot. Oh, he did get some mystery phone call, now I come to think of it. Rang me to know if I'd been trying to contact him, I said no, I hadn't . . ."

"When was this?"

"That afternoon. The fellow you want is the one who made the call."

"Ever owned a pistol, Mr. Lamb?"

"Not even an air gun. And if you don't believe me you can take the house apart. You'll have to square Mrs. Worth, but I expect you know all about that."

"You suggested it, not us," said the policeman smoothly.

"You mean—you've got a search warrant?"

"Do we need one?"

"My landlady's particular. She likes everything left tidy. There she comes," he added. "Visitors, Ma," he called over the banisters. "Things are coming to a pretty pass when you can't even call your home your own."

"Where have you been all these years?" demanded Mrs. Worth. "Years since anyone could do that. You in trouble?" she added crisply.

"Just a routine call," said one of the policemen.

"Nothing to do with me," asserted Terry.

"Then you've nothing to worry about, have you?"

But that wasn't true. Because he was made to realize he might have quite a lot to worry about. When he was asked about his alibi all he could tell them was that he'd had a couple of drinks at a pub called the Kingfisher before he went along to collect his load from Mr. Moss.

"You mean that's where you were at the time Mr. Crook was shot?"

He saw the trap there and by-passed it. "What time would that be?"

"Well, impossible to be absolutely certain, but the doctor thinks around seven-thirty."

Terry thought. "About that time I'd have been in the Kingfisher at Lake."

"They'd remember you there, I expect," suggested the sergeant cordially.

Terry favored him with a sullen glare. "No reason why they should. I didn't break up the bar or anything."

"Still, if you're a regular . . ."

"I didn't say that."

"My mistake. I understood . . ."

"There's no law says you have to go to the same pub every night. Matter of fact, it's only about the third time I've ever been there."

"I see. Any particular reason?"

"There's only one reason I know for going to a pub, and that's to get a drink."

"Didn't happen to see anyone there you knew?"

"There wasn't anyone there I knew."

"The barman now," insinuated the sergeant.

"I'd never set eyes on him before. He'd only been there three weeks, I heard two chaps nattering. The other one had married into the trade and was helping in his father-in-law's bar."

"Doing good business?" asked the sergeant casually.

Terry shrugged. "Places like the Kingfisher are like those supermarkets, people trickle in for a pint and out again, like moving on an escalator."

"I suppose you didn't go there to meet anyone?"

"I told you, I went in for a drink, I didn't see anyone I know, and so far as I'm aware, no one saw me."

"I see."

"I bet you do. A whole lot of things that aren't there." Terry was getting rattled; he gave himself a mental shake. You're okay. No witnesses. No proof. "How much longer is this going on?" he demanded. "If you've quite finished I'll be getting on with my own business."

"Why, it's only just gone six o'clock, Mr. Lamb. You can't be wanted this early."

"I can't go on an empty stomach, can I?"

"We'd be glad if you'd come down to the station," the sergeant said. "The inspector would like a word . . ."

"Are you taking me in?" asked Terry dangerously.

"Why on earth should you think that? No, it's your safety we're concerned about. If you don't know anything about this Crook affair, and you say you don't, then whoever is responsible might take a pot shot at you. Had you thought of that?"

The officers thought they were used to variegated forms of speech, but the constable said later he'd never heard a colorful storm of invective such as Terry treated them to now. "He even used some four-letter words I didn't know existed," he acknowledged.

But for all their skill they couldn't break down Terry Lamb. Crook could have told him there are three answers to a police interrogation. I don't know. I wasn't there. Everything went blank. Ring the changes on these and Bob's your uncle. No one had told Terry this, but he had a natural sense of self-preservation.

"Crook's right," said Inspector Mount—because eventually Terry went with them as they'd intended all along. "That chap knows more than he's saying. There are times," he added wistfully, "when I remember countries where you can use the third degree to get the information you want. I suppose they're keeping an eye on Dr. Gray; I get a notion he might be able to help us yet."

At seven o'clock Terry was still maintaining an obstinate silence. It wasn't much of an outlook for Mr. Moss, who might have to get a substitute driver at precious short notice. At seven-five Dr. Gray left the Moor Park Nursing Home, where he'd spent the afternoon dragging a patient back from the Gates of Death.

"He'll do," he told Matron. "Whether he'll be so grateful when he comes round and realizes the sort of life we've saved for him is another matter."

"Any sort of life is better than none," urged Matron, and he sent her a dark glance.

"I wonder." From her office he rang his own house. "Any calls, Mrs. Thrupp?"

He always rang before setting out on his homeward journey, and if it was humanly possible Mrs. Thrupp always said firmly there was nothing urgent.

And that was what she said tonight. "Nothing urgent, Doctor." No mention of maddening Mrs. Ray, who as a private patient rang up whenever she had a stomach ache or a pain in her big toe, and would have expected the doctor to come beetling round through a thunderstorm or a tidal wave. Mrs. Ray had already telephoned twice, to be told by Mrs. Thrupp that she couldn't say when Dr. Gray would be back, he was operating, but the message would be passed on. And so it would, but not till the doctor had had a breather and a whiskey-and-soda and a chance to tackle a meal. Poor man, it wasn't much of a life, Mrs. Thrupp thought. She herself didn't sleep in, which suited both of them; she preserved her independence and would have a home to fall back on if anything happened—if, say, he collapsed from overwork, as well he might. A man needed a wife, Mrs. Thrupp thought, it kept him human. No one admired Dr. Gray more than she did, but men weren't intended to live this inhuman existence. He was a devotee of his job, but the personal element was lacking. He doesn't have any fun was the way she summed it up, though she couldn't imagine what form his fun would take. She put out the drinks and fetched his slippers—she was cooking one of his favorite meals, so far as he ever preferred one dish to another. And then the phone rang again.

"If it's that Mrs. Ray," she told herself violently, lifting the receiver, "I shall say he's had a stroke. A woman like that's enough to give any man a stroke."

But it wasn't the tiresome Mrs. Ray, it was a man speaking in a voice she didn't recognize, though she prided herself on being able to distinguish most of Doctor's regulars on the telephone.

"Doctor isn't in," she said firmly. "In any case there's no surgery tonight."

"Is that his wife?" the voice asked, very deep, unsympathetic.

"This is his housekeeper, I'm used to taking his messages," she said coldly. "I can't say when Doctor will be back, but if he's not home by the time I go I'll leave a message on his desk."

She looked at the clock. It was seven-fifteen. He was due back in fifteen minutes, unless something happened to detain him.

"You do that," the voice agreed. "But be sure you put it where he'll see it."

Her tone was more glacial still as she assured him, "I shall put it with the other messages. He'll get it all right."

"I wouldn't want him to miss it. It's important."

She sighed impatiently; they were all important, according to the speakers.

"Just say that if he knows what's good for him he'll keep out of other people's affairs, unless he wants to go the same way as Mr. Crook, that is."

Mrs. Thrupp gasped. Whatever she'd anticipated, it hadn't been this. She knew what had happened to Mr. Crook, of course. It had been on the wireless, though what Crook had to do with Dr. Gray was anyone's guess. She'd never so much as heard him mention the name.

"Who's speaking?" she demanded when she had got her breath back.

"He'll know," the voice assured her, and she heard the sound of the receiver being reslung. She hung up her own instrument in a state of considerable agitation. It wasn't right, threatening a man who gave all his life to his fellows. As for Mr. Crook, why couldn't he stay in his proper place, instead of gallivanting all over England, getting decent men into danger? She ran to the door and opened it, listening for the sound of the doctor's car, but she knew it was too soon. By rights he shouldn't be operating in a nursing home so far from his own neighborhood, but that was him all over, never thinking of himself. She shut the door and came back into the house. For a minute or so she remained deep in thought. Then, with a defiant toss of her sandy head, she picked up the telephone receiver and dialed the police.

Dr. Gray came in just before the half-hour, his complexion suiting his name. Mrs. Thrupp decided to say nothing about the caller until he'd had a drink and a chance to get his breath back. Any sane man would ring the police at once, but you could never count on what the doctor would do. She'd have liked to wait till after he'd had his dinner, but there was always the chance the authorities would ring back or even call round, and he must be prepared. But she fussed around him so much that he must have smelled a rat, because after a few minutes he said, "What on earth is it, woman? You're as jumpy as a flea in a gale of wind." So she told him—but only about the call.

Dr. Gray's reaction was disappointing. "Some maniac, I suppose," he said.

"Maniacs can be very dangerous," she pointed out. "And why Mr. Crook?"

"Why not?" asked Dr. Gray.

"Shouldn't you report it to the police?" she ventured, and he stared.

"Make myself the laughingstock of the neighborhood because I've had an anonymous call?"

"He sounded as if he meant it."

"He sounded like that last time, but nothing happened."

She goggled. "You mean this isn't the first!"

"That's just what I mean. No, I can't tell you who he is, someone who doesn't think he got enough attention, perhaps, someone I told was scrimshanking—but if he meant to come round with his little popgun he wouldn't have rung up to warn me first."

"Mr. Crook," she began, and he cut in, "There's no record of any mystery call being made to him."

"Well, we don't know, do we? Unless he's been able to tell the police . . ."

"Is there any fresh news about him?"

"There was a bit on the six o'clock. He's off the danger list."

"Then he's the man for the police to contact." He set down his glass. "Sure there were no other messages?"

"Only Mrs. Ray, and you know what she is."

"I'll ring her back later," the doctor promised.

"You can't go out again," she began, and he turned and stared. But before either of them could say another word the front doorbell rang.

"Who on earth . . . ?" the doctor began. "My surgery hours are stated clearly enough on my plate."

"Perhaps it's him," faltered Mrs. Thrupp.

"Come to shoot me down in the presence of a witness?" He laughed; he actually laughed. "Well, hadn't you better see who it is, or would you prefer me . . . ?"

She scuttled to the door, opened it, and there they stood, two policemen as large as life. She'd never been more pleased to see anyone.

"Oh, come in," she said quickly. "Come in. Doctor's just back."

Gray, hearing voices, came into the hall. "What's all this?"

"We hear you had an anonymous phone call," one of them told him.

"How on earth did you know? Mrs. Thrupp, did you . . . ?"

"Yes, I did," said Mrs. Thrupp defiantly. "That man meant what he said, you can always tell."

The doctor sighed. "I'm afraid you've been brought out on a fool's errand," he said, "but come in." He didn't make the mistake of offering them drinks, he knew they weren't allowed to drink on duty. "I've only just heard about the call," he explained. "I've not been back more than a few minutes."

"I daresay you were going to ring us yourself, sir."

"Frankly, I wasn't. If I'd got on to the police every time I've had an anonymous threat . . ."

"You can't suggest who can have made it?"

The doctor shrugged. "Calls are being made by madmen every night, often to people they've never met and have nothing against."

"But you're not suggesting this was one of those? I mean, there was a mention of Mr. Crook."

"Seeing that everyone appears to be talking about him, that's probably the first name that popped into the fellow's mind. I don't see how you can hope to trace a call like that . . ."

"It came from a public call box," Mrs. Thrupp put in. "They say they always do, the anonymous ones, I mean."

"Well, there you are," said Gray, as though that explained everything.

"What time was this?"

The doctor looked at his housekeeper. "About a quarter past seven, soon after you rang from the home," she said.

"Obviously the chap wasn't on my tail or he'd have known I wouldn't be here."

"He'd have known your housekeeper was, though, or he wouldn't have bothered to put the call through. Have you any suggestions as to who could have made it? Mr. Crook has recovered enough to make a statement—he had a call, too, only he was out at the time."

"Did he, then? And this chap put his threat into practice? If you're tying up this call with the Crook shooting, then there's only one name that occurs to me, and that's drawing a bow at a venture. I've no proof whatsoever that this man could be concerned."

"Who would that be, sir?"

"I'm surprised Crook hasn't told you himself. Or perhaps he has. All right, then. There was a lorry driver called Terry Lamb in the lane on the night the girl was killed, at approximately the right time and place."

"And Mr. Crook knew this?"

"I told him."

"I don't recollect that the police . . ."

"I didn't tell anyone else."

Mrs. Thrupp's face was a study, but everyone seemed to have forgotten her.

"You're quite sure, sir? That could be important."

"I'm dead sure. Mind you, Crook told me he hadn't mentioned me by name to Lamb . . ."

"But he knew there was someone who could give evidence?"

"That's about the size of it."

Mrs. Thrupp said, "Why don't you tell them you had a call before this one?"

"Also anonymous," the doctor agreed. "It's dangerous to make a statement you can't support."

"You think that may have been Lamb, too?"

"It's only a suggestion."

"It must have been him," Mrs. Thrupp burst out.

"I don't know about the first time," the policeman said, "but it can't have been Lamb tonight. It was seven-fifteen when you rang the station . . ." He looked interrogatively at the housekeeper, who nodded. "Well, Lamb had been in our hands for over an hour when that call was made. And I don't think you'll find they'd allow him to use the station phone."

"Besides," put in the other policeman, speaking for the first time, "the lady said it came from a call box."

"I heard the pips," Mrs. Thrupp averred.

"So you see, sir"—they both turned toward the doctor—"we'll have to look elsewhere. And we were wondering if you'd feel inclined, though you don't have to volunteer a statement or even answer our questions, not without advice"—the appalled Mrs. Thrupp heard the familiar words of the police caution roll out on the quiet air—"wondered if you'd care to tell us who you were ringing from the call box on the Pendragon Road at seven-fifteen tonight?"

XIII

"I DON'T BELIEVE IT," said Mrs. Thrupp in anguished tones, after they'd taken the doctor away. "It can't be true, not him." She walked up and down her room like a creature in a cage, oblivious to the lodger below, who banged frantically on the ceiling with a broomstick. "Giving his life away all the time, he'd never hurt a girl or an old woman . . ."

Up and down she went, knowing the police were wrong and trying to find a way to prove it.

"What on earth put you on to the doctor?" Terry Lamb demanded of a convalescent Mr. Crook, raring to go back to London with its comparative security and the bright lights of home. "And why have me pulled in? Honest, I thought I was for the high jump."

"Serve you right if you had been," said Mr. Crook unsympathetically. "Know who I'm glad not to be? And that's the girl you're going to marry."

"Not if old man Moss can help it," retorted Terry grimly. "I've had my cards and a note to say not to ask for a reference and Sally's gone to stay with her auntie in Bournemouth and no letters will be forwarded."

"Bournemouth's not such a big place," Crook soothed him. "It could have been South Africa. If you'd told me the truth from the start . . ."

"That was likely, wasn't it? If I'd come forward I'd have found myself in the nick in record time, and heading for the gallows—well, a life sentence—before you could say knife. I'd only got to let on to the police that I'd seen the girl that night and given her

169

a lift—what put you on to it, anyway?"

"You told me yourself," Crook assured him. "You said she was skinny and looked no more than sixteen. So she was skinny, but no one had actually said so, not in the press anyhow, so how did you know? And she did look young for her age, but you never got that out of the papers either. And then I didn't think the doctor invented the place where he saw the lorry. It was Marigold Bottom, whatever you may say."

"I said the lorry broke down about a mile further on, and so she did," Terry insisted. "She hadn't broken down when the doctor saw her. I'd stopped her to try and prevent that little fool committing suicide. Honest, Mr. Crook, she should never have been let out on her own."

"She wasn't let out," Crook reminded him. "She ran off . . ."

"Because there was a party and she wasn't invited. Well, it was a grown-up persons' party."

"Isn't eighteen grown-up?" Crook sounded scandalised.

"I told you, she didn't look eighteen or anything like it. I didn't believe her when she told me. If I'd known I mightn't have stopped for her, but I thought she was just a schoolkid who didn't know enough to stay away from the lane that time of night. I couldn't believe my eyes when I came round the corner and there she was, inching along by the hedge like a field mouse or something. Of course I knew the rules about picking up birds, you can't blame the bosses, really. Only this wasn't a bird, this one hadn't got the sense she was born with. You'll think me daft, Mr. Crook, but I felt responsible. Funny, I'd never have felt that before I met Sally. Staggers you sometimes what a girl can do to you." He brooded.

"I've heard lorry drivers described as the Knights of the Road," contributed Mr. Crook obligingly.

Terry disposed of Knights of the Road in a couple of well-chosen syllables.

"I went right by her but a minute later I found myself stopping. I put on a fag, then as she came inching up I opened the door of the cab and said, Where do you think you're going, darling? This is a pretty good road to Nowhere. She put her nose in the air, and it wasn't the sort of nose made for that kind of thing, and she said, That just shows you don't know your way about. This is a short cut to the Halt. I'm going to catch the London train. You're joking, I told her, that train goes out in forty minutes and it's all of three miles. If you think you can do that on your own plates of meat . . . All right, she said, then I shall catch the next one. You'll be waiting a long time, I told her, and they shut the station. What do you want to go to London for this hour of the night anyway? I had a message, she told me. And I told her, Pull the other one, it's got bells on. She said, Oughtn't you to be getting along? Isn't anyone expecting you? Well, I told her, if they are it's more than you can say. What about your people? Aren't they going to worry? And she laughed. Honest, Mr. Crook, it gave me the shivers, a laugh like that. Whatever they're worrying about, it won't be me. And anyway I've left a note. Who do you know in London? I asked her. And she said, I don't see that it's any business of yours, but I have an aunt. Funny sort of aunt who expects you to turn out in the middle of the night, I said. Now look, I'll tell you what I'll do. I'll give you a lift to the end of the lane, that way you might catch your connection. I wasn't going to take her right on to the main road, I wasn't going to chance any of the chaps seeing me giving a bird a lift. They've got a funny sense of duty, some of them, and tongues a mile long. You must think me stupid, says the young lady, which was just what I was thinking, of course. Do me a favor, I told her, it's no skin off my nose if you're found in the morning in a ditch with your throat cut, but your auntie's going to be upset, isn't she?" Terry paused; he shuddered.

Mr. Crook said impatiently, "This is the kind of story you want to hear in a bar, with all the appropriate trimmings, not in a refined prison cell." He looked disconsolately around the spotless hospital room. "Well, go on, I suppose you persuaded her at last."

"Only after I'd assured her that if the old man found out about it he'd probably give me my cards. She made that quite clear. All right, she said, just to the end of the lane. I suppose it is true what you said. You're a bit of a big girl for anyone to have to start making up fairy tales for you, I told her."

"She sounds a gracious young lady," offered Crook.

"Born the wrong side of the bed and so got out the wrong side. I tried to find out something about her, but she wasn't talking. Won't they wonder about you at school tomorrow? I asked her. And she said, Don't be silly, I left school ages ago. Don't try and kid me you're more than sixteen, I told her and she said, I'm eighteen. Mind you, I still didn't believe her. Well, well, I said, who'd have guessed? Now I've got an idea, there's a phone box round the next corner, why don't we stop and you can ring your mum and they can come and fetch you. Much better than hanging about waiting for a train you probably won't catch anyway. I've told you, she said, they're at this party, goodness knows what time they'll get back. And they won't worry, he isn't even my father. Well, I thought, poor little devil, is her stepfather making himself a hell of a bore? Only you couldn't believe that. I mean, she wasn't the type. It wasn't just that she wasn't a looker, lots of girls aren't beautiful, but there was something missing—you can always tell. No—no warmth," concluded Terry desperately.

"What really made you pick her up?" asked Crook, and he really wanted to know.

"Well, as much on Sally's account as anything. I thought, Supposing it were Sally coming down the lane on her Jack Jones this hour of the night? Did you know I was the one who found the old chap they cut up with bicycle chains just for a giggle and the fiver he had in his pocket? Chaps who'll do that wouldn't have made any more of knocking this girl around than they would of kicking a kitten to death. Suddenly she's struggling to stand up. Stop the lorry, she commanded. I want to get down. Don't be a juggins, I told her. We aren't anywhere near the station yet. I've changed my mind, she said, I don't want to ride with you any longer. That got my dander up. You'll get down when we get to the main road and not before, I told her. Anyone 'ud think you were a little tramp. I expect you're used to that kind, she said. If you don't stop at once I shall tell the police how you offered me a lift, made me come up—and they'll know why, there's only one reason really. That made me hopping mad, even without Sally . . ."

"Okay," said Crook, "you've made your point. Well?"

"It was just about then that the motorcycle came zooming up

behind us. We both heard it, and she opened her mouth to yell. No, you don't, I said, and I got her face jammed against my shoulder with one hand over her mouth. She bit me like a little animal—I had to explain the scar to Sally, a little cat, I told her, got stuck in a tree, couldn't get up, couldn't get down. I don't know whether she believed me. After that I felt I didn't care if a cannibal tribe came out of the bushes and ate her inch by inch. As soon as the bike was out of hearing—the chap never looked in our direction and I don't think he could have seen her if he had—I stopped the lorry and told her she could go to bloody perdition her own way. And I hope you enjoy yourself when you get there, I said. I hurled her little case down at her and she dashed off through a gap in the hedge, and of course I had to remember just where we were. The Bottom's a treacherous sort of place, specially if you don't know your way around, and the mood she was in she could go tip over arse into the bog and probably wouldn't have the sense to pick herself up again. Mind you, it's not all that deep, but there was an old chap suffocated there a couple of years ago. He'd had a skinful, and when he fell down he couldn't get up. Don't go that way, I yelled, not unless you're set on suicide, and I got down from the lorry and went pelting after her. I could have broken her neck with pleasure. Of course, she decided I was chasing her to rip off her pants and have me a ball; she wouldn't have listened to an archangel, if there'd been one handy. Well, I couldn't stop her and I didn't want to find myself accused of chasing her into the bog, so I stopped and said, For God's sake, look where you're going, that's all. I did think I might send a call from the phone box, I don't know, perhaps I wouldn't, but when I came out I got into the lorry—if your doctor pal was hanging around, I never saw him—and went off hell for leather."

"That's what he says," Crook agreed.

"So he did see me?"

"He saw you all right, but not, he says, so he'd know you again."

"I'd forgotten Daisy was a lady and you have to treat them delicate; we hadn't gone far before we came to a dead stop. I'm pretty nifty with my hands, but that night I couldn't do a thing.

There didn't seem anyone coming either way, so I walked on to the phone booth and tried St. George's Garage, which is where we mostly go. But they didn't answer and nor did another one I tried, and I didn't know any others, and of course there wasn't an A.A. man anywhere, even if he'd been allowed to help, which probably he wasn't."

"So in the end you got her going on your own account?"

"I told you before, didn't I? Anyway, it was Hobson's choice. I wasn't sure I'd make the market, she was quite likely to lie down again, but we got there just on time. Joe had packed up and gone home by the time we reached his stand, but I wouldn't have been able to stop anyway. Of course, next day he wanted to know what had happened. I didn't think about the girl again till I saw the piece in the paper about her being found in the wood, probably died on the Monday night. That shook me a bit, I can tell you."

"Didn't think of going to the police?" Mr. Crook suggested.

"I didn't think of anything else, but I didn't go. Well, would you? I didn't know who'd done it, who she'd met. I never saw anyone who could have been responsible, but do you suppose the police would have believed me?"

"Can't blame 'em really," murmured Mr. Crook in temperate tones.

"Oh, sod that!" cried Terry. "Matter of fact, it was the other chaps who made up my mind for me. See about that girl, Terry? they chaffed me. I suppose you didn't meet up with her? Terry's a man of mystery, they said, and one of them noticed my bad finger. Oh, a cat did that, I told them, a little cat caught in a tree . . . So of course Galahad to the rescue, that southerner, Williams, had to say. I could have crowned him. Why don't chaps stay in their own part of the world? Was it a lady cat? they asked. All good clean fun, I daresay, but a bit too near the bone for me. And then they started tying up that death with the old woman at the Poets House."

"You couldn't have told them about anything about that," Crook agreed.

"Ah, but I hadn't any alibi, hadn't spoken to anyone at a garage, hadn't met a soul on the road—even Joe couldn't testify to what time I went roaring past. I might just have been able to fit in a couple of murders before I delivered the goods. Mr. Crook, what made you think it might be the doctor?"

"You gave me my first trump," acknowledged Crook handsomely, "though I didn't know it at the time. When you said it was rum that a chap who only used the lane about twice a year should be so darned certain where he'd pulled up. On a dark night, too. Are you reading me?"

"Well, not loud and clear," Terry confessed.

"You said the hedges were so tall you couldn't have seen the girl on the further side, not from the road, not if she'd been walking there . . ."

"So how did he know there was this great marsh of marigolds on the other side unless . . ." Terry paused, staring.

"That's what I call reading me loud and clear," Crook told him.

"But—but why? Or is he one of those chaps . . . ?"

"He's not one of those chaps, but he's something almost as dangerous, he's a doctor, and what's more he's a doctor with a sense of vocation—to go on with his job of doctoring."

"What's wrong with that?" Terry inquired.

"Say you couldn't go on driving a lorry for some inexplicable reason, what'd you do?" Crook inquired.

"That's different. I'd get another job. Shouldn't be too hard."

"That was Dr. Gray's trouble. To him there wasn't anything but doctoring—if he couldn't do that he was finished. And since he believed it was important to the world that he should go on being a doctor, at any price you could name . . ."

"You're having me on," Terry accused him. "Do you mean you know . . . ?"

"He's made a full statement now, and I've been told the gist of it."

"Wonder how they got that out of him," said Terry cynically.

"He told them," said Crook. "Yes, of course he did. They didn't have to winkle the facts out of him with a hot iron. And he ain't walking about in sackcloth and ashes. To him it's a case of the end justifying the means. A hysterical girl—though that was an accident, we have to give him that—a dying old woman, me, if need be you, all obstacles in the way of the work he had to do."

"Get along!" murmured Terry. "He doesn't hate himself much, does he?"

"He's like a lot of these do-gooders, lose all sense of proportion. The girl was a misfit, the old woman was dying, if I wasn't it was about time I thought about it, you . . ."

"I suppose you could argue his life was worth more than mine," agreed Terry handsomely. "To the community, I mean."

"Well, it won't be for the next twenty years," was Crook's brutal retort. "Even chaps in chokey are going to think twice before taking anything from his hand."

"You still haven't said where he comes into it."

"He takes up the story where you leave it off. He told the truth up to a point. He did turn into the lane because he was feeling shaken and didn't want to get involved in an accident, he did stop to light a cigarette, and he did find he hadn't got any matches. He waited behind your lorry, expecting you to turn up any minute, but when you did you came out like the Wrath of God, jumped into the cab and went off like a cat with a tin can tied to its tail. And about half a minute later this girl appeared in the gap in the hedge, mopping and mowing like a maniac."

"I heard a lot of commotion," Terry acknowledged, "but I didn't look round, I'd heard about enough. According to her she'd been raped and abused, lucky to have escaped with her life. And she was going to tell everyone . . ."

"That's what she was yelling and Gray reacted as any doctor would. He went over to find out what was wrong and see what he could do about it. He told her he was a doctor. But she was beyond listening to reason, she just screeched at him not another, keep back—you can imagine the sort of thing."

"I don't have to, mate," said Terry feelingly. "You're forgetting. I was there."

"Then while he was still trying to calm her down he heard a sound, like a car coming out of the wood. And she heard it at the same time. She turned to shout for help, and he did the obvious thing, tried to shut her up. It was an ugly situation for him, a professional man of his age alone in a wood with a hysterical girl—unmarried men of his generation are always a bit suspect."

"Hark who's talking!" ejaculated Terry.

"Oh, I don't count," Crook assured him comfortably. "The girls take one look at me and start remembering the last time they were at the zoo. But there'd been that incident with the first lorry driver, who might be prepared to come forward and say he was driving under the influence anyway, and in a case like this the girl gets all the sympathy, and it's her story that's believed. It could spell ruin for the doctor, so he does just what you did yourself. Put his hand over her mouth, just to keep her quiet till the intruder's gone by. Not a particularly enviable situation even so, but it's not likely he'll be recognized, he's off his own stamping grounds here, and it'll be another case of a petting party in not very salubrious surroundings. Only it don't work out that way. The girl had this status lymphaticus—that means that a normal pressure or any shock that wouldn't seriously affect chaps like you and me could put paid to her account. And that, in fact, is what it had done."

"Poor old bugger!" said Terry kindly. "Only goes to show what happens when you try to do someone a good turn."

"Must have been a shock," Crook agreed, secretly admiring the way the young can take the most outrageous situation in their stride. "When a young woman who's been literally kicking and screaming in your arms one minute turns into a sack of nothing the next. He hadn't much time to decide what to do. He couldn't afford to be seen hanging on to her, and anyway a corpse"—Mr. Crook shook his big red head—"anyway he stuffed her under the bushes, hoping to get away with it, perhaps, but when he turned, there was the old black dragon coming over the hill, and an old woman's voice was calling, What's going on? What's wrong? Can I be of assistance? Well, it was too late to pretend everything was smooth as ice cream, so he went forward and asked her if she'd seen anyone during the last two or three minutes. Only you, she said, but I heard a girl's voice, she seemed in distress. She was in distress all right, he told her, I heard her voice from the lane. Then he said he was a doctor, he'd come into the wood—it was darkish, it was one of those nights, if you remember, with the moon dodging in and out of clouds, and mostly out when you'd have preferred her in—and then he said, I don't want to alarm you unduly, but there's been an outrage committed, there's a dead girl under the bush there. That's why I asked if you'd seen anyone, because whoever is responsible can't be very far away."

"Kept his wits about him, didn't he?" Terry offered.

"Probably suffering from delayed shock himself. That sharpens the wits wonderfully. Mind you, he must have known he was on pretty thin ice. Grown murderers don't disappear into thin air, and there hadn't been any sound of footsteps. And then if the girl had been bawling a minute before, only he'd stopped her before she got into full cry, she'd got herself stowed under a bush in double-quick time. Still, the old lady mightn't think of all that. So he said, The police must be informed, and she suggested he should stay with the girl while she went back to the Poets House and called them. Only he wasn't going to have that. He didn't know what she'd say, he didn't know how much she'd seen, so he said he thought it was dangerous for her to go on alone with the murderer hanging around—all poppycock, of course."

"You mean he'd already made up his mind to do for her—in cold blood?"

Even Terry seemed appalled at last.

"He says no, not then. He was going to tell the police the truth, that he'd seen you go bolting out of the wood and then the girl dashing after you, and—it was established, you know, that she was virgo intacta, not even any attempt made at interference, but all the same, that kind of story has a nasty smell."

"Do you mind," began Terry ominously, but Crook swept on, "It was when they got to the house and he saw Mrs. Nick clearly for the first time that the details began to fall into place. Mind you, he could well be believed about not knowing the girl, not making any attempt against her virtue, but it ain't enough to be innocent, you must be obviously innocent to everyone, and quite a lot of people were going to wonder what he was doing in a place like the lane that hour of the night. Like I told you, he had to be like Caesar's wife."

"What was so special about her?" Terry asked.

"She had to be beyond reproach, and not only be but appear. In the old days a Spanish gent could cut his wife's throat if there was even a whisper about her, though there might be no substance to it. The whisper was enough."

"A lot of wogs," said Terry comfortably.

"Like I said, it wasn't till they got inside the house that he saw Mrs. Nick clearly, and being a doctor he realized at once that she was a dying woman, not in the same sense that we're all dying men and women, but . . ."

"Ready to conk out any minute?"

"Did she seem that way to you?"

"Be your age, mate, I never saw her."

"No, of course not. And nor did I. And if we had the odds are we wouldn't have known. Because those who did see her, P.C. Doyle and Mrs. Fred and even her buddy Miss Jewell—none of them had any notion she had this disease, Howard's disease it's called. It was Dr. Morton who put me on to it, but it was Gray himself who told me, and I didn't hear. He said a hysterical girl and a diseased old woman. But how did he know she was diseased when none of her neighbors knew?"

"Because he was a doctor, you said it yourself."

"But he wasn't supposed to have met her," howled Crook. "He couldn't have known unless he'd seen her. She didn't have a professional doctor, and if she had, it wouldn't have been him. But Morton says any doctor would have recognized the symptons. The niece she was going to stay with, her husband's doctor, he'd have known. He told me that," repeated Crook in a voice of horrified amazement, "and it was like water off a duck's back. It was only when Morton repeated it . . ."

"What happened?" Terry inquired. "You mean he slugged her?"

"I couldn't have put it better myself," murmured Crook. "According to him he had reason on his side. No one could do anything for the girl, and he didn't feel any guilt about her, and why should be? He'd only wanted to help—and here he was, an able, a dedicated man with another twenty years of solid work ahead, and it was all going to pot because an old woman who'd got about three months left was going to testify against him."

"How do you make that out? I thought you said he didn't know . . ."

"That's just it. He didn't know—how much she'd seen, how much she'd deduced. More to the point, what the police would deduce. If he told his story it put you in the clear, so far as the girl's death was concerned, but who was going to be the better off for that? And say the old girl had topped the rise a second or two before he knew it, and saw him struggling with her—he hadn't got any life but his work, and if he lost that he might as well put his head in a gas oven. And once the story started going round he'd be finished, he knew it. Probably even convinced himself that he owed it to the world to stay on the job, at any cost to any other person."

Terry knitted his brows. "You mean he was a real nutter?"

"He was a chap who believed in destiny," said Crook solemnly, "and himself in charge of it. When he said would she like to put the call through, seeing the local police knew her and she needn't worry because she really knew nothing, had seen nothing, she said, I shall tell them everything I know—naturally. And I hope they will take it up at once, as I'm sure they will, as I'm due to leave the house tomorrow, my niece is expecting me, I have a car laid on, et cetera. If she'd wanted to commit suicide she couldn't have done it neater. And so," he wound up, "when she lifted the receiver Gray came up behind her, the phone's in the hall there, and knocked her out. Quite a professional job, I believe. An amateur, once started, wouldn't have known where to stop. It's a funny thing, they get a sort of compulsion, once they've struck the first blow . . . Then he dumped her in the car, a good idea really, seeing the neighbors knew she wouldn't be taking it with her, rang the niece, rang the garage—a doctor attending Mrs. Nick, sorry she wouldn't be able to travel in the morning, no, she couldn't come to the phone. All truth, you see. And finally he moved out, no reason why his name should ever be associated with the case. Then home, James, no one to make a note of time of arrival, he lives on his owney-oh, no one to wonder why it should take him so long to get from the hospital to his own place. Even when the bodies are found, why should anyone think a Dr. Gray was involved? Then the police took Frankie Piper, that must have been a relief to him . . ."

"It was to me," said Terry candidly. "Mind you, I thought he must be the right chap, been in the old woman's house . . . I don't carry any banners for the police, but it must have seemed a dead cinch."

"Very coincidental evidence," Crook agreed politely.

"And no sense me coming forward, because she was alive and kicking when I saw her and I didn't see anyone else. What made your doctor come out of hiding? Wouldn't he have shown more sense to live low?"

"Well, of course he would," said Crook. "But it's the curse of the age. Everyone wanting to play safe. Suppose someone had gone along the lane while he was away and had noticed his car, might even have noticed the number, then when they started asking questions about the girl the informant might have surfaced. So long as everyone believed it was Frankie, he was all right, but then I appeared and he began to get cold feet. He knew, he must have known, I wasn't going to let Frankie stay on the spot, so I'd be looking around for someone else. And there were you, nice and handy. Only, of course, he couldn't tell me he knew you'd been there without letting on that he'd been there himself. He didn't suppose anybody could establish a case against you—the benefit of the doubt, that was what he said. The fact that there had been another chap on the spot would get Frankie the benefit of the doubt. What he didn't know was that once you start on the downward path, there's no stopping. It's like a runaway lorry, once it's out of control you have to go with it, and if someone get in its way and gets hurt, that's just too bad."

"In this case, meaning you?"

"If you meet a lion in the way, there's only two things you can do about it," Crook acknowledged handsomely. "You can tame it, same like St. Francis, or you can put a bullet behind its ear. It could be Dr. Gray hasn't had much experience of taming wild beasts, anyway he opted for the bullet. A nasty shock for him when I put up my head and called Boo. A gentleman would have died to preserve the Gray tradition, but I ain't no gent. Even the police, who have called me a lot of things in their time, have never called me that."

"And all these fancy phone calls—did he make those?"

"Oh, I think so. Who else was there—except yourself? Mind you, the one he told me he'd had was just a fantasy, but he was the one who rang me when Mrs. Fred took the message, and he sent himself a call that last night from the box on the Pendragon Road. It's an old fallacy and I'm surprised he fell for it. Chaps argue that if they're getting threats that puts 'em in the clear. Like sending yourself anonymous letters."

"And now?" Terry said.

"Are you asking me? The girl's out for the count, the old lady ditto, the doctor'll be behind bars for the rest of his natural, I'm on my way to London, that nice safe city where you do know where you are, and you're headed for Bournemouth—right?"

Terry grinned. "You never give up, do you, mate?"

Decisive steps sounded in the corridor outside. A firm resonant voice said, "You have no right to be here, I have assured you . . ."

"I've every right," interrupted another voice, equally resonant and full of the bright scorn of youth. "Just you try keeping me out. I'll come down the chimney if I have to . . ."

Terry rushed to the door and pulled it open. "Sally!"

"You must have told Mr. Crook your life story four times over," said Sally Moss. "I only wish I could have listened in. I bet you told him a lot you've never told me."

Terry said "Sally!" again in a stupefied sort of voice, and Matron broke in, "If this young woman is here on your account, will you kindly take her away at once. It is a flagrant breach of regulations . . ." But the regulations had been flagrantly breached ever since Crook's arrival.

"Well, you can't win them all, can you?" said Terry. "And Mr. Crook's so used to having his own way— That was a record flight from Bournemouth," he added to Sally.

"You really thought I'd gone there? If you'll believe that you'll believe anything. You ape, you didn't really think you were going to get off that easy?"

"Your father," Terry began.

"I thought it was me you were proposing for, not the family business."

"Hey," interrupted Crook, "you sound like a married couple already. Nice to think you both knew what you were doing, mostly they don't and by the time they come to realize it, it's too late."

"You might thank Mr. Crook for saving your life," Sally suggested.

Terry put his hands in his pockets. "Shouldn't you be doing

that?" Neither of them took the least notice of Matron.

Sally went over and held out her hand. "It may seem odd to you, but I am grateful," she said. "Mind you, I thought I was marrying a driver, not a knight-errant . . ."

"Not to worry," soothed Crook, "in no time at all you'll find you've just got a husband, like all the rest."

"I've been a lot of bother to you, haven't I, Matron?" said Crook when the young couple had departed. "So you'll be relieved to know I'm planning to take my leave in the morning, say."

"Nonsense!" retorted Matron briskly. "You'll remain where you are until you are discharged by the doctor, and that will not be for some days yet. There's been enough publicity about this case without your collapsing as soon as you leave the premises. And there has been a telephone call," she added, "from a Mrs. Ann Piper. She wishes to know whether she can bring a case against the police, or rather if her husband can, for wrongful arrest, and if so, what damages she could claim."

"You're joking," said Crook feebly. "Even the female of the species can't be that wacky. The police just did their job . . ."

"I am glad to hear you say so."

"Did you say she was going to descend on me?" inquired Crook weakly.

"No, Mr. Crook, that is what she said. I informed her you were seeing no visitors in connection with business until the doctor gave you permission. I reminded her that you have a partner in London . . ."

Crook lay back against the pillows; he looked rather like the Rock of Gibraltar rolled over on its side.

"Perhaps you're right. Perhaps I should take things a bit easy for the next day or two," he murmured. "I'll have a word with Bill. He won't like it, I'm afraid, but it's what Terry Lamb said just now—you can't win 'em all."